"I Don't Like Horror Movies."

"I'm not scared of them," I lie as coolly as I can. "I just think they're stupid. Give me one good reason why anybody goes to see them."

Rosalie steps forward with a definite leer on her face. "Revenge! Listen, didn't you ever just want to kill somebody? Maybe one of your parents, or your brother or sister, or some teacher or kid who's been bugging you to death? You can't do it, of course. But you can fantasize about it. Just think of giving them the treatment you saw in the latest horror movie. Lady, I wanna tell you, *that* is satisfying!"

Rosalie is watching me closely. "Agreed then? Let's go!"

MARLEEN THE HORROR QUEEN

Lila Perl

AN ARCHWAY PAPERBACK
Published by POCKET BOOKS
New York   London   Toronto   Sydney   Tokyo   Singapore

An Archway Paperback published by
POCKET BOOKS, a division of Simon & Schuster Inc.
1230 Avenue of the Americas, New York, NY 10020

Copyright © 1985 by Lila Perl
Cover art copyright © 1987 Catherine Huerta

ISBN: 0-671-73484-9

First Archway Paperback printing January 1987

10 9 8 7 6 5 4 3 2

AN ARCHWAY PAPERBACK and colophon are
registered trademarks of Simon & Schuster Inc.

Printed in the U.S.A.

IL 7+

Contents

1

My Mother, the Jock

IT'S A QUARTER past eight on a sultry July morning. The sun is like hot butter. And here comes my mother, the jock.

She's wearing a tank top and running shorts. Her coarse, reddish hair has been chopped off close to her head, and her freckles have melted into the sweaty redness of the rest of her skin.

I'm looking out the window of our second-floor garden apartment, set deep, deep in a courtyard filled with parched grass and scraggly bushes, cracked concrete paths, and benches. Lots of benches.

Two long arms of apartments, two stories high, reach out and enclose the courtyard forming a giant U. This place is a goldfish bowl! The benches and paths are empty right now. But the long arms have eyes. The neighbors are watching through their windows, standing back just a little, the way I am, so they won't be seen. But I know what they're thinking.

"This dame is nuts," they're thinking. "Every morning in ninety-eight-degree weather, she gets out

1

there at six-thirty A.M. and runs for an hour and a half. What's she trying to prove?''

Sure, I know everybody runs these days. In all kinds of weather. But wait, you don't know the whole story about my mother. She's into this thing called female bodybuilding. She lifts weights. She works out with dumbbells and barbells. She pumps iron.

She's at the Y gym or the health club every day, both keeping herself in shape and teaching classes. She even gives private lessons to women who want to enter those body-beautiful contests, flexing their muscles for the judges.

Actually, she's won a couple of trophies herself, flashing and rippling her biceps and triceps. It's both an art and a science, she tells me, learning how to develop the female musculature to improve fitness and enhance one's appearance. Really ugly bulges, she insists, are not what she's after. But I still think she's got too many muscle bumps on her arms and legs, and her neck is too sinewy. It embarrasses me the way people—teenage kids especially—look at her.

Barefoot, I go slouching into the kitchen in my shorty nightgown as she comes hip-hipping it up the stairs. The more energy she has, the tireder I get. Maybe I'm just having a reaction.

"Marleen," she pants, "not dressed yet?"

She's still keeping to her pace as she races off toward the shower. I can imagine her in there, prancing up and down like some punch-drunk prizefighter under the slick needles of water.

She pads briskly into the kitchen wrapped in white Turkish towels, her big reddish face glowing with health, her dark berrylike eyes snapping.

Now comes her liquid breakfast—Tiger's Milk, with

2

soy concentrate and brewer's yeast in it. She'll add a couple of fertile eggs, some granulated seaweed, lecithin, bone meal, carob powder, maybe some raw sugar or honey, and a few more magic potions from the health-food store.

Everything whirls dizzyingly in the blender. Then she brings the milky froth to the table and sits down for the first time this morning.

As I sip my orange juice, I can't help thinking how much things have changed in the six months since she and I moved here to Westchester, just north of New York City, from the New Jersey shore.

Sure enough, she looks across the table at me and says, "What are you thinking, babe?"

I lie, of course, though only a little.

"I'm thinking it would be great to get in the water today," I say. "Just get wet and stay wet. All day."

"You can," she says. "Come to the Y with me."

"Ugh," I reply. "An indoor pool. That stink of chlorine. No air to breathe. No clean, salty breeze. How can you stand it, after all those years of living near the ocean?"

She winces slightly. "The ocean's nice for playing. Pool swimming is better exercise."

I hunch my shoulders. "Ma, I don't want to exercise. I *want* to play. It's my school vacation. Nearly a whole week since school closed, and all I've done is mope around this apartment, do a little baby-sitting, and perspire a lot."

Also, I don't bother to add, I don't have any friends. The school crowd seems to have vanished for the summer, and the only older kid in the court is Alex Kirby, who's fifteen and won't look at me.

"Your choice, Marleen," she reminds me. "I told

3

you you could go back any time. I'm not trying to split up the family."

But you *are,* I scream silently. Lately I'm having all these double conversations, saying what I really think to myself and the polite thing to other people.

The truth is that my parents are having a "trial separation." Nobody calls it that but me. Nobody calls it anything, really. But six months ago, my mom got an offer to work at a fancy health club in New York. It has branches, including one in this big mall in Westchester, but none down on the Jersey shore where we lived.

She grabbed it. "Let's all move," she'd said, brimming with energy, as though she were just starting off a calisthenics class.

My brother, Neil, who is sixteen and three years older than I, looked at her as though she were crazy. He had a bunch of friends, an old jalopy that he and my pop were fixing up, and he worked summers at the town beach. In the seaside sun, his skin turned a warm, toasty tan, and each golden hair on his legs and arms flickered like a tiny flame. The girls adored him and he knew it.

Alex Kirby, this kid in our court, looks so much like Neil it's weird. I keep wondering if he's as conceited, if he thinks all girls are pushovers, soft in the head, the way my brother does.

I *know* Alex thinks my mother is strange. Two mornings ago as she came chugging into the court, I looked out the window and caught him and his older brother, Ace, standing on their doorstep and snickering, their heads together. It gave me a sick-in-the-stomach feeling. I didn't know who I was angrier at, my mother for making a spectacle of herself or Alex

4

and his brother for looking at her like that. Oh how I wish I could get away from this place.

My mother seems to be reading my thoughts again this morning. "Tell you what," she says. "We'll compromise. You'll swim in the pool today and we'll go home to the ocean for the weekend."

"Really? You mean it?" I'm beginning to feel a tiny bit better already.

Since January, when we moved north, we've gone home to visit every five or six weeks, whenever Mom could get a weekend off from the health club. Maybe she works off her guilt toward Pop and Neil that way. She checks out the house, cooks, cleans, does some laundry. I don't know where she gets the energy, between the long drive down and back. Maybe there's something in Tiger's Milk after all.

Mom's just finishing the last of her breakfast concoction. She glances at the kitchen clock. "Come on, kiddie. Get dressed. I'll drop you at the Y pool. I have a bodybuilding group at nine."

Mom's always in a hurry, always meeting a schedule. "Chop-chop." That's one of her favorite expressions.

I shrug okay. I guess I might as well. Nobody's phoned about a baby-sitting job for today, and it's stifling in this apartment under its sun-baked roof. It'll be nice getting down to the shore for the weekend, our first hot-weather visit since we left there. It'll be nice seeing Pop and *maybe* even Neil again.

Why do big brothers always act so superior and indifferent, if not downright mean? Ever since Neil got to be such a hotshot around town, such a big number with the girls, he began to grow more and more distant toward me.

Something else happened too. He got to be closer to Pop. I began to feel shut out. I was sure Pop loved me. I'd always adored him. But I think that as I grew older, entered my teens, maybe Pop didn't feel that comfortable around me.

By the time Mom made her decision to take the new job and move, Pop and Neil had become buddies. I knew Neil told Pop about his girlfriends. But if I stumbled in on them, their private, high-pitched laughter stopped instantly. I was a girl, after all, so I guess I was the enemy.

Mom hadn't twisted my arm about coming with her to Westchester. She didn't need to. And even though she'd said I could "go back any time," I didn't feel I could. So in a way of course, and even though she'd denied it hotly, she certainly *was* splitting up the family.

Just getting myself into a bathing suit and a pair of jeans is torture in this sticky heat. Mom looks fresh, though, in clean white shorts and a tee-shirt. We lock the apartment door and clatter down the stairs to the courtyard. Oddly enough it's still deserted. The benches are empty, and the usual beach chairs haven't appeared on the little paved squares in front of the apartment stoops. Not even Mrs. Hofmeier, a sprawling white-haired lady who boasts of being an "original resident," is holding court this morning. It's that hot.

We lope around to the parking lot behind one of the long arms of the U. I always breathe a little easier when I'm outside the fishbowl. As we approach Mom's car, an old load that somehow keeps going on spit and prayers, a huge moving truck grinds into the lot.

"Hmmm, new neighbors," Mom says brightly.

"Or maybe somebody's moving out," I suggest hopefully. Alex Kirby, I think to myself, remembering his twisted smile the other morning as he and his brother stared openly at Mom. I'd been sort of admiring Alex up to then, thinking how he might turn out to be a nicer version of Neil and a sort of friend, or even boyfriend, for the summer. Now I wouldn't have minded seeing the last of him.

Mom shrugs as she opens the car door. "Thirty-two apartments in the court. Who can keep track?"

"Some people can," I answer pointedly. "Some people keep track of everything."

But Mom isn't getting the message. She's blithely winding down the windows, starting the engine, steering her way around the moving truck.

"Drive fast," I say, as we pull away. "Don't stop until we get there." With movement there's a breeze at least. Hot as a blowtorch, but a breeze.

We're about six blocks from the apartment when Mom suddenly stops the car. There's no red light, no traffic jam, the engine hasn't failed.

"What's wrong?" I demand. "Did we forget something?"

Mom's squinting toward the intersection.

"Somebody's stuck," she replies.

I follow her glance. There's a car about as old as ours smack in the middle of the crossing. A figure is seated at the wheel, steering, and another one is behind the car trying to push it.

"They're on an incline," she remarks. "They're going to need help."

I look at her with impatience. That's another thing about my mom. She's a Good Samaritan. "Oh no," I groan. "It's so hot. And you'll be late for your nine o'clock class if you stop."

But she's already pulled over to the curb and is opening her door. "People have helped me so many times," she says. "It's the right thing to do, Marleen."

I look around. There *are* other cars passing. Some nice strong man might get out and help. But no, my mom, Mrs. Muscles, has to do it.

Should I go too? I feel so stupid. I'm scrawny and flat-chested in my bathing suit top. My arms are long and milky-colored next to Mom's brawny freckled ones.

Slowly I open the door and get out. Mom's already far ahead of me, approaching the car on the run. I amble along in no hurry. I don't know who these people in the car are, but I'm not that anxious to get up close and present myself as the daughter of Wonder Woman.

Already Mom's taken her place next to the person who's pushing. Her knees are pumping, her body is straining, and now the car is starting to move up the incline and across the intersection. There's something familiar about the car, like I've seen it somewhere before. Or is it just because it's a maroon-colored old load that looks so much like ours?

Mom's figure is blocking that of the other pusher, but I'm close enough now to see the person who's sitting at the wheel, steering. I expected it to be a woman or maybe an older man. But it's a kid, somebody who's maybe even too young to drive. A thrill of horror goes through me as I realize who it is. It's the

8

last person on earth I would want it to be. It's Alex Kirby!

Instantly I know why the car looked familiar. I've seen it around the court. It belongs to Alex's brother, Ace. I don't need to know another thing. The person my mother is pushing the car with is Ace himself, a swaggering seventeen-year-old with a smirking mouth and a bleak, cold stare.

At that moment Alex spots me through the driver's window. He's never even glanced my way before, but now it seems perfectly clear he knows who I am.

I'm the jock-woman's daughter.

Right away he starts shaking his head back and forth gleefully, laughing with ridicule, and thumbing a finger in the direction of my mother at the rear of the car. "Well," he taunts, in a croaky, insinuating voice, "don't-cha think you oughtta go and lend a hand back there, little lady? Shouldn't let your old mom do it all, ya know."

I've halted a short distance from the car, mortified and speechless. So this is what Alex Kirby is like up close. I feel as if I've been smacked hard right between the eyes. To think I ever had any romantic fantasies about him!

Alex is staring at my bathing suit top now. His gaze travels from my pale, skinny neck to my waist and back again. Instinctively I cross my arms over my chest and clutch at my shoulders with desperate hands. Why can't I think of anything to say? Why am I standing here letting myself be more and more humiliated?

"Nah," Alex remarks, shaking his head as if he's having a conversation with himself, which actually he

9

is. "I can see you're not the type for heavy jobs." He gives me a slit-eyed look, full of secret amusement. "No biceps." He wags his head again. "Nope. Nothin'."

My anger explodes in a piercing flash of hatred. "You . . . CREEP!" I cry out hoarsely.

Mom, who has stopped pushing for the moment, looks up with surprise at the sound of my voice. But she does nothing about coming to my defense. Instead, she rearranges her stance and braces herself for the final shove that will propel the Kirby car to a safe spot beside the curb.

I turn at once and run back to our sweltering car. Even after I've climbed inside and shut the door, I'm sure I can hear the sound of Alex's mocking laughter following me. I sit there, cascading with sweat, rocking back and forth, waiting for my mother to return so I can tell her what fools she's made of us both.

Why, oh why, did she have to stop to push that car in the first place? And why, of all cars, did it have to turn out to be the Kirby boys' car?

I jam my fingers into my mouth and bite down hard on my knuckles. So I've met Alex Kirby at last. I won't ever forget how horrible he was. And I'm not forgetting either that this whole ugly encounter would never have taken place if it hadn't been for my mother, the jock!

2

This Kid Rosalie

BOBBIE AND I aren't talking. My mother's real name is
Roberta, but everybody calls her Bobbie. I always
think of her as Bobbie when I'm mad at her. It's a
man's name after all, and isn't that what she's trying to
be?

I'm not against equality between men and women. I
think it's fine if a woman wants to be a firefighter or a
police officer or go to West Point. But not *everybody*
thinks like that. And it's the way she flaunts those
muscles of hers that really gets to me. Can't she see
how embarrassing it is? Back home in New Jersey my
mother was quieter about her physical toughness, it
seemed to me. And then, too, people in town knew her
since she was a tomboy kid. They just accepted her.

But here in this garden-apartment development it's
all nosybody new neighbors, little clusters of sharp-
eyed, sharp-tongued women, and that two-faced Mrs.
Hofmeier. "Had a nice run this morning, Mrs. Hubbell?" she says every time she sees Mom. "It's wonderful the way you keep in shape."

Those veined blue eyes, though, are full of doubt

and disapproval and questions. Where is Mr. Hubbell, eh? And what about this skinny, gangly Marleen who flits about like a wraith and looks the exact opposite of her muscular mother?

Sure enough Mrs. Hofmeier is sitting out as I sneak back into the court just around lunchtime. Refusing to let Mom pick me up at the Y after my swim, I've taken a bus and walked the rest of the way. The pool was okay, but how long can you sit around inhaling chlorine fumes and feeling like you're inside a tank? I think I'll get into a cool tub and read this afternoon. Bobbie won't be back from the health club until suppertime.

"You look wrung out, dear," Mrs. Hofmeier sniffs. I *have* to pass her to get to our front door. "Been walking?"

I nod, moving as fast as I can.

"Wait!" Mrs. Hofmeier commands.

Her voice is so sharp I actually stop dead in my tracks. The women, some with small children, sitting and chatting around Mrs. Hofmeier all give her their attention. I feel like I'm going to be called to account for something. Probably this morning's humiliating incident of Mom's pushing Ace Kirby's car. Could the Kirby boys already have been shooting off their mouths about that crazy Mrs. Hubbell?

I look around nervously, anxious to get upstairs to the safety of the apartment.

Mrs. Hofmeier points with a bony finger. "Look over there."

I follow her direction down the long right arm of the court. The doorway to one of the apartments is wide open and just then a couple of moving men are coming out. They stoop to gather up the ropes and protective quilts they've been using to haul furniture. I've completely forgotten about the moving truck that Bobbie and I saw pulling into the parking lot this morning.

"New people have just moved in," Mrs. Hofmeier reports. "The old Berringer apartment. Of course, you wouldn't know. The new folks have a girl about your age. I've already talked to her. Nice chum for you. I'll send her over in a little while, now you're home."

The women, young and old, around Mrs. Hofmeier nod approvingly. Everything's been arranged, it seems. Oh, this place is even worse than I thought it was. I never noticed it so much through the winter and while school was in session. It's a tiny kingdom full of fawning gossiping subjects, with Mrs. Hofmeier reigning over them like an aging queen. What will happen when she dies? Will the next oldest "original resident" take up the line of succession?

"Thanks," I nod dumbly as I turn and flee up the steps. What else can I do?

I've been in the apartment only a few minutes, checking out the unflavored yogurt, alfalfa sprouts, and wheat-germ bread that Bobbie keeps in the refrigerator and wondering what to have for lunch, when there's a sharp rap on the door.

I open it without even bothering to ask who it is. The next moment I jump back in alarm. I'm confronted with a midget wearing dark glasses and dressed in a black halter top and an ankle-length gypsy skirt. She's wearing a purple headband around a thatch of creased-looking mouse brown hair. For some reason I notice she's got on clunky brown sandals and her toenails are painted green.

"I'm Rosalie," she announces bluntly. "Just moved in. The biddy with the white hair sent me."

"I figured," I say, trying to play it as cool as she. "Name's Marleen."

She grunts. Of course Mrs. Hofmeier has already told her that.

"Can I come in?" she says, already pushing past me and peering into the living room. "I'd like to find out right away if you're weird enough for me. So far I'm not impressed."

I back away helplessly and let her into the sparsely furnished living room. "This is good," she remarks. "Not too conventional."

Most of the stuff in the room is actually old wicker porch furniture, repainted and the cushions recovered, that Bobbie had kept stored in the attic back home. The rug is a sort of oversized fiber mat. We don't have visitors, so it doesn't seem to matter much. The bedrooms are even barer.

Now that Rosalie's in the apartment, I realize she isn't a midget, just normally short and with a pale, pudgy face and shoulders. I wonder how Mrs. Hofmeier figured out she was around thirteen. In that getup she could be twenty-eight, thirty-five, forty-two.

Rosalie's heading for one of the wicker porch chairs when she trips over the edge of the fiber rug and nearly lands on her chin. The tail of her skirt flips up in the air and she cries out, "Ufff!"

"Watch it," I say hastily. "You'd see better without those dark glasses."

"Sez you," she replies, flopping down hard on the flowered cotton-print cushion of the chair. Her glasses have slipped to the tip of her nose. But she only pushes them back up to the bridge with her middle finger. "They're prescription. But forget I told you."

I sit down on the edge of the sofa opposite and we sort of stare at each other.

"Who else lives here?" she demands, looking straight at me with those black, impersonal lenses.

"Just Bobbie and me," I respond. Let her figure that one out.

"Your dog? Father? Brother?" She's still very cool. Nearly falling on her face hasn't ruffled her at all.

Rosalie's looking for "weird," so I'll do my best. "My mother," I reply. "Otherwise known as Mrs. Muscles. She's at the gym right now having a workout. Great biceps." Even as I say these words, I feel an ugly twinge of pain, thinking of Alex Kirby's comment on *my* "biceps" this morning.

Rosalie just nods, leaning back in her chair. She's so short that her feet, green toenails and all, come up off the floor. "Nice," she says. "You've got two points so far."

I curl up on the sofa, my legs under me. "How many to be weird enough to be your friend?" I challenge her. "And why would I want to be anyway?"

"Because," she says, suddenly looking very solemn and very wise, "you need me."

"Maybe," I suggest, "it's the other way around."

I've never before met a kid like this Rosalie and I've never played this kind of game with anybody. Her air of superiority is both comical and infuriating. Who does she think she is anyway, this twerp in the crazy outfit? And where does she get her nerve? She's newer than I am in the court, and *she's* interviewing me.

Rosalie just shakes her head. "Friends," she says. "I've got dozens. Scores."

"Not around here," I tell her. "And you won't.

15

Maybe you haven't taken a good look yet. If Mrs. Hofmeier sent you up to meet me, it's only because she figures I'm your one chance for a friend. So how come *you* get to do the picking?"

"Because," she answers mysteriously, "that's the way it is. What makes you think I care if I have a friend in this court or not? My family's not going to be living here very long. It's just a perch for us between houses."

"Between houses?" I repeat. "What's that supposed to mean?"

"What I said," she replies. "My dad owns this big plumbing supply business in town and my mom volunteers at the thrift shop down near the railway station. We just sold our house, and then the deal unexpectedly fell through on the one we were going to buy. So we put a lot of stuff in storage and rented an apartment here until we find another house. We might only stay a month or two."

That explains in part why Rosalie can afford to be so independent. But there's still a lot to answer for concerning her strange appearance. I'm anxious to know what the rest of her family looks like. But I guess I'll find that out soon enough. Nothing remains a secret very long in the court.

All the time we've been talking to each other—or maybe it should be called taunting each other—I've been noticing that Rosalie's purple headband has been getting darker and darker. Now it can't even hold the droplets of sweat any longer. Her eyebrows are glistening.

"Listen," I say, "it's pretty hot up here. I'd offer you a glass of fig and pomegranate juice, but I don't think there's much left. How about yogurt with garlic and cucumber juice? There's no Coke or anything like that in the house. My mom's a health nut."

Rosalie grins. "Three points. You made it!" She leaps up from the chair. "Congratulations. Though the credit really goes to your mother. I'll look forward to meeting her."

I remain sitting on the sofa. "Wonderful," I say sarcastically. "So I'm weird enough for you. Now what happens?"

"Now," Rosalie declares, heading for the door, "I think of something great for us to do this afternoon. Something chilling and satisfying."

"Really? What did you have in mind?" I'm still pretty miffed by her attitude. What makes her think I'm ready to be *her* friend, to fall in with *her* plans for the day? Am I supposed to be so grateful for her approval that I should get down on the floor and kiss her green toenails?

Rosalie whirls around to face me. She clicks her fingers in the air. "Simple. There's a horror movie playing in town that I haven't seen yet. We hitch a ride in, grab a double-cheese pizza, and then cool off with the creeps." She consults an oversized watch on her wrist. "Be ready in ten minutes. Meet you down in the court. And bring money."

I'm on my feet in an instant. "Whoa. Hold on a minute."

Even if I liked everything about Rosalie, I'd still have plenty of objections. For one thing, I'm not supposed to hitch rides. And thumbing down cars with somebody dressed like Rosalie would be asking for trouble. I can just see us climbing into one of those

17

curtained vans and ending up a pair of dismembered bodies, with Rosalie's green toenails sticking up out of a sandpit.

"Hitching's out," I tell her firmly. "And besides I don't like horror movies."

Rosalie bares her teeth in an evil smile. "Ach, zo," she says in a phony accent, "a case of jelly in the knees, eh?"

"I'm not scared of them," I lie, as coolly as I can. "I just think they're stupid. I can't see why anybody goes to them. Give me one good reason."

Rosalie steps forward with a definite leer on her face. "One good reason? Revenge!"

I look at her slightly startled. "Revenge? On who?"

She shrugs. "Whoever. Listen, didn't you ever just want to *kill* somebody? Maybe one of your parents, or your brother or sister, or some teacher or kid who's been bugging you to death? You can't do it, of course. But you *can* fantasize about it. Just think of giving them the treatment you saw in the latest horror movie. Lady, I wanna tell you *that* is satisfying."

I watch her, mesmerized. Does she have any idea how close she is to what's been on my mind lately? Ever since this morning, I've been especially wishing I could think of some way of getting even with Alex Kirby for the way he looked at me and the things he said. As angry as I am at Bobbie, I'm hundreds of times angrier at him.

Rosalie is watching me carefully. She's got some uncanny sixth sense about me. I've been feeling that from the moment she walked in the door.

She comes over and claps a pudgy hand up onto my shoulder. "Agreed then? Oh, and when I said 'hitch,' I didn't mean 'hitch' hitch. I'll get somebody I know to drive us. Trust me."

This kid Rosalie. I've been talking to a pair of shiny black lenses the whole time. I don't even *know* if she has eyes. And she looks like a dress-up bag lady or an escapee from a Halloween party.

Yet, I somehow do trust her. So I decide I'll scribble a note for Bobbie saying where I've gone, and I agree to meet Rosalie down in the court in ten minutes. With money.

3

Revenge!

WHAT A MOVIE! It wasn't one horror story; it was four.

One of the episodes, of course, *had* to be about the living dead returning from the grave to take revenge. In another, a married woman and her boyfriend were buried up to their necks in quicksand by the woman's husband. Then slowly, slowly, they watched the tide come in.

The third horror tale was about a mechanical hand, a sort of Frankenstein's monster, that had a mind of its own. It kept coming back to get even with its mad-scientist maker. And the last story was the most gruesome of all. It was about a brilliant chemist who figured out a bug-killing spray that backfired. It turned whatever insect it was aimed at into a people-eating monster, zillions of times its original size.

I had planned to sit through the horror movie without so much as a twinge. I wasn't going to let on to Rosalie if I was scared or sickened, if my knees turned to jelly or my belly to mush.

But of course it didn't work. When we came out into the sizzling late-afternoon sunshine, I noticed at once that Rosalie's left arm and hand were blotched red with pinches and scratches where I'd grabbed her in moments of terror.

She caught my look, lifted her arm, and just grinned. For some reason, her face looked naked and I found myself peering into a pair of large velvety brown eyes through clear-colored glass. Rosalie, too, must have realized something was wrong. She reached quickly into her skirt pocket and took out the prescription sunglasses she'd been wearing until we'd gotten inside the dark movie theater, where she'd sneakily changed them for the clear ones.

"You have nice eyes," I told her. I felt I'd had a quick glimpse of the real Rosalie. "Why don't you leave the clear glasses on?"

"Nobody has nice eyes behind glasses," she snapped back, "and I can't wear contacts. Besides, this getup is my *schtick*. I'm working on having a style of my own." Her eyes completely vanished behind the black lenses. "So," she went on without a pause, "what did you think of the movie? Aside from what you recorded on my arm, kiddo."

"I know one thing," I replied. "I'm not spraying another mosquito this summer, or even a fly. Those man-eating cockroaches. Brrr." I shuddered. Rosalie had been right about cooling off in the hot weather with a horror movie. I was still having chills.

"Ahh," she declared, "that movie was adolescent junk. Wait until I get you to a revival of *The Body Snatcher* or *Isle of the Dead*. Then you'll know what it feels like to have ice water in your veins. By the way, did you get any good ideas for revenge?"

I looked at her in surprise. What made her think I was thinking of revenge? I'd never admitted to any such thing, and I'd never said a word to her about Alex Kirby. Sometimes Rosalie herself gave me the creeps. And yet I also felt sort of protected by her. Maybe it was just her being so weird, weirder than any kid I'd ever known.

We got back to the court the same way we'd come. Rosalie's mother drove us. She was small and slightly pudgy like Rosalie, but an absolutely normal-looking woman, wearing perfectly ordinary clothes. If she thought her daughter was a little far-out, she certainly wasn't letting on about it. I told myself there was a whole lot about Rosalie that still needed explaining.

It's early Saturday morning and Mom and I are in the car headed for the Jersey shore.

"We'll get there by eleven easily," she assures me. "Plenty of time for a dip before lunch."

I nod. Mom and I are speaking again. But there's still a gap of cautious politeness between us. As long as we each stay on our side of the slowly narrowing abyss, we feel safe.

"I wonder how Pop and Neil are making out," I say, just to add my share to the conversation. Mom phones home, usually from the health-club office, a couple of times a week, so we're really not that out of touch.

Mom laughs. "Oh, the house'll be the usual mess, I suppose. Empty soup cans in the kitchen, TV-dinner trays in the living room." She's trying to make it all sound as lighthearted as one of those situation comedies on television.

Mom's love affair with health food hasn't rubbed off

one little bit on Pop and Neil. They're strictly the burger-and-fries type. And I won't exactly mind eating some of their "poison" for a couple of days. Mom isn't taking any chances, though. She's got a canvas satchel in the back seat loaded with vitamin supplements, dried seaweed, and alfalfa capsules to tide her over the weekend.

Mom rolls the window all the way down and starts humming a little tune. The wind blows freely through the car. We're on the Garden State Parkway heading south and I'm waiting to sniff the first hint of a salt breeze from the ocean, somewhere over to our left.

It feels good to be going home, good to have a whole long, lazy summer stretching out ahead of me, good to think of seeing Pop and even Neil again. Pop's slow-moving, relaxed, easy to be with. There's none of that tension I always feel around Bobbie. And the guilt that I'm not *doing* something for my body. Pop's a good summertime person.

Maybe, I think to myself, I'll even stay on for a couple of weeks and let Mom return by herself. I can go back on the bus any time really.

Mom glances over at me. "Feeling better?" she wants to know. There's something a little more personal in her tone.

"I'm fine," I say cheerfully. And then I spill my thoughts. "Maybe I'll even stay down home awhile. How would that be?"

I'm watching Bobbie's profile at the wheel. Her jaw tightens slightly. I'm sure of it.

"Okay if you want to," she says in an even voice. "I thought you had a new friend you liked in the court."

I haven't told Mom much about Rosalie, only that we went to a movie together. "I'm not sure she's my type," I reply. "She's sort of far-out."

"How?" Mom asks.

"Oh, she's got weird tastes. And she's bossy. Anyhow, she says she isn't going to be living there very long. Maybe only a month or two."

Mom shrugs. "I'm sorry you feel the way you do about the court, Marleen. I don't find it bad at all."

"That's because you're hardly ever around," I reply. "And even when you are, you're not."

The car gives a sudden jolt. "What's that supposed to mean?" Bobbie's face is reddening. "Are you going to get back on those two boys again? I still feel I helped them out of a rough spot. If they can't appreciate a favor, if they want to act like a couple of male chauvinist pigs, that's their problem. I still don't see why you're so upset."

I glare stonily at the road ahead and say nothing.

"The older one, the one I was pushing with, said 'thanks,' " Bobbie points out. "If he and the younger one made faces behind my back, who cares? I've been in athletics all my life, Marleen. I can throw my weight around too. It's time some more of these ignorant characters found that out."

"You can't change how kids are," I say in a flat voice. "They make fun of anyone that's . . . that's different. And teenage boys have to feel they're the greatest. You should know that from . . . from the way Neil is. That Ace Kirby. He's seventeen and he thinks he's tough. You made him feel like a . . . a sissy. Maybe he didn't have the strength to push the car uphill all by himself. But if it was a man who'd come along and helped him, it would have been better."

Bobbie's driving faster now, her eyes fixed tautly on the road. "Let me tell you something, babe. I don't go for that male superiority stuff and I never will. You know, when I started out in female bodybuilding it was a young sport. And it still is, compared to male body-building. You never had a chance to see me competing at any of the championships, but you've seen photos. The women wear bikinis and they have to be skimpy ones so the judges can see the musculature. And of course all the contestants coat their bodies with oil to highlight the muscles."

I nod grudgingly, thinking of Bobbie's album of poses. In some of the pictures she's proudly holding one of the trophies she's won. I shudder to think of what Alex and Ace Kirby would say if they ever saw those shots of Mrs. Muscles.

"Well," Bobbie goes on, "at one of those early contests, the audience wasn't used to seeing women compete and they thought they were watching a beauty pageant, Miss America or some such thing. They began calling out, making really disgusting remarks, like we were so much meat on display. They said personal things that were very belittling to women, things they'd never say to the male contestants."

I'm squirming with embarrassment now. Why is Bobbie rehashing all of this?

"The judges weren't about to stand for that," Bobbie says firmly. "They stopped the judging and one of them went to the microphone. He said some of the best things I've ever heard about respect for athletic events, respect for the sport, respect for all participants. After that, there was silence. The judging went on and you could have heard a pin drop. By the way, I won third place in the Northeastern Women's Division that day. It was no small triumph."

I sigh. Bobbie is so self-satisfied. She's not the one who's being hurt by her actions. I am. Why can't she see that?

"That happened *then,*" I comment. "It won't make it any easier for me the next time I have to face that kid Alex or his brother back in the court. And that Mrs. Hofmeier is the queen of the gossips. I hate the way she looks at me."

"You're just suffering from teenage self-consciousness," Bobbie remarks, as she slows the car down for one of the parkway rest stops. "It's perfectly natural at your age. I *do* sympathize, baby. But can I change my entire life-style?"

Bobbie pulls neatly into a parking space near the restaurant and snack bar section of the rest-stop complex. She turns to me with a serious look. The flesh between her eyebrows crinkles into three perfect vertical creases, straight as arrows. "I've told you this before, Marleen, but I'll say it again. You'd find it a lot easier to deal with your problems if you took up an interest, like a good strong hobby or a sport."

Like *you,* I think to myself. This is useless. We're just going around in circles. And it's stifling sitting in this parked car for even one extra minute.

Can't Bobbie see that I'm not like her and that I don't want to be? I don't answer her and, without another word, she gets out of the car and heads for the rest rooms. I follow sullenly.

Bobbie is walking directly in front of me. She's wearing shorts and a halter and she's doing her muscle-flexing as she walks, getting the kinks out after two hours of steady driving. Muscles are suddenly bulging out of nowhere all over her arms and legs, like pop-overs. They ripple, pop, and disappear. Then new ones come to the surface. Even I'm fascinated. It's no small feat to be able to do this.

Is it my imagination or are people turning to look at her? A couple of older teenagers are coming toward us, a well-built boy jangling car keys and a beautiful willowy girl with long dark hair. They see Bobbie, and the moment she passes them they stop and stare with curiosity. They have no idea that I, dawdling behind, have any connection with her.

"What was *that?*" the girl asks in a giggly whisper. They're watching Bobbie's back now where the same strange ripplings and poppings are taking place.

The boy grins and scratches his head. "Beats me," he replies. "Lady wrestler, maybe? Weird."

Shrugging their shoulders and snickering softly, their heads together, they stroll past me just as the swinging door of the ladies' room closes behind Bob-bie.

I slink by them, no expression at all on my face. But my head is filled with vengeful thoughts, and I'm pulsating with helpless anger. How I hate all these staring twosomes with their snide looks and insulting remarks. Suddenly I have this great vision right out of Rosalie's horror movie.

I see a lonely beach, the waves pounding at the shore and the sun beating down mercilessly. Two people—I'm not even sure who they are—have been buried up to their necks in the sand. Their pleas for salvation have been useless. They know they will not be pardoned, that they will never escape. Their mouths are bound with gags. Sharp-beaked seabirds are swooping low above their heads. And, like the pair in the movie, they watch with horror as slowly, slowly, the tide rolls in . . .

I punch at the swinging door and enter the ladies' room with a secret smile on my face. I'm thinking of what Rosalie said about how satisfying it is to fantasize getting back at people who make you mad. And she was right, absolutely right. Revenge *is* sweet.

4

On the Beach

NEIL HAS A new girlfriend. Her name is Yolanda. She's fourteen, only a year older than I, but I can't believe it. Will I ever be as self-assured and sophisticated, as slender yet curvy? Will my wan, light brown hair ever be as sun-streaked, wavy, thick, and stunningly cut as Yolanda's?

We're all at the beach this Saturday afternoon—Neil, Yolanda, Mom, me, and even Pop has come along. It's like a family reunion, so peaceful and cosy. Mom is snoozing, facedown, on a blanket stretched out in the sun. Neil, who's off-duty this hour from his job as life-guard's assistant, is about to take off with Yolanda for a stroll down the beach—"Maybe all the way to Cape May," he says with a suggestive wink as they amble away hand in hand.

That's a joke of course. Cape May is at the southern tip of New Jersey. It's miles and miles. But he wants us to know they'll be gone awhile, and maybe they'll be up to something. Yolanda just smiles. I can't make out whether her smile is knowing or vacant. How do *I* know what kids like Neil and Yolanda do when they're off by themselves? Nobody ever tells you the truth, and it embarrasses me to think about it. If my turn ever comes, what will I do?

Pop's in a lounge chair under our faded old beach umbrella. And I'm on the sand sharing the shade with him. We're both fair-skinned and we burn easily. Pop's wearing his regular trousers and shirt and reading the sports page. He's not big on swimming and stuff. Fishing and maybe a little hunting are more in his line. So, in a way, I feel he's come to the beach today in honor of Mom and me being home for the weekend. And that's nice.

I often wonder how Pop really feels about this arrangement my mom has worked out. Is it supposed to be permanent, or what? When Mom had said, "Let's all move," she'd known perfectly well my father wouldn't go for it. He was too comfortable where he was. And what about Pop's business, a TV and stereo repair shop that was right in his own backyard? Actually it was in an expanded shed attached to our house. It was so convenient that Pop could just roll out of bed mornings and take care of customers. Other times, he went on neighborly house calls around town to work on ailing TVs that were too big to be brought into the shop.

"Me move?" Pop had said. "What for? An old country doctor doesn't leave his practice after years of building it up. Folks around here depend on me."

FRED HUBBELL, THE TV DOCTOR—VIDEO, AUDIO, STEREO, & RADIO REPAIRS. That's how Pop advertised his business. "Electronics is just like the human body," Pop was fond of saying. "Always something going on the blink. My patients'll keep me going for years."

The "old" in "old country doctor" had really gotten to my mother that day when she'd proposed moving. "Old at forty-two," she'd said with exasperation. She was vigorously rubbing a towel through her freshly washed hair. "Too old to make a change. Aren't you ashamed?"

Pop had just grinned good-naturedly. "You go try this health-club job if you want to, Bobbie. Go try it," he'd said calmly. "Sooner or later, you'll be back."

Mom had flashed him a look. She threw the towel around her shoulders and grabbed the edges tightly with her fists. She looked funny, her short red hair sticking up in spikes and curlicues, but nobody laughed, not even Neil. "Old at forty-two," she'd repeated. "But then sometimes, Fred, I think you've been old for a long time now. Too much TV, I'd say, from *both* sides of the screen."

She politely didn't mention on that occasion, as she usually did, the beer that went with Pop's TV watching and the fleshy belly he'd been getting from his evenings of home entertainment.

All in all, I guess they'd been slowly growing apart for quite a while. The easier Pop seemed to take things, the more Mom had thrown herself into her bodybuilding. It was what she was good at. And when the offer to make some money with it came along, she wasn't going to let her big chance pass her by.

My parents must have come to some sort of agreement. No fights. At least, not any that I heard. And the rest just fell into place. Neil would stay behind with Pop. I'd go with Mom.

But this weekend, so far, everything feels like old times. Even Neil seems friendlier. The sounds on the

31

uncrowded beach are just wonderful—the lulling, swishing noise of the ocean, the distant cries of gulls and children and faraway swimmers. Even the sun seems to be humming. Bobbie hasn't stirred. She's a short distance away, but I can hear her steady breathing punctuated every now and then by the faintest of snorts.

I hoist myself up to lean on the arm of Pop's chair. The sports page comes down and he grins at me. "Hey, Marleen," he says gently. "How's my girl?"

I nod happily. I want him to know that I still love him and I'm glad to be here. I'm afraid words will spoil it. I want him to know that I haven't deserted him. Just in case he thinks I have.

He reaches out and smoothes back my hair where I've cut some short ends that I hoped would curl around my forehead in becoming tendrils. So far they haven't.

"Nice day, huh?" Pop comments. "I hope that answering machine back at the shop isn't fouling up again. Could be some business coming in."

"Oh, business," I remark. I don't want to talk about that. Still, maybe it's a good opening for me, for what I do want to talk about.

"Hey listen, Pop," I say, thrusting forward a little, "I'll bet you could use a good secretary this summer. Part time, of course. Because I *would* like to get to the beach now and then . . ."

The sports page drops with a crackle alongside the chair and Pop's eyebrows go up. He smiles a little sheepishly. "What are you talking about, sugar?"

The more I think about my sudden idea, the better I like it. I really could make myself useful to Pop answering phones, keeping records. If Pop said he needed me, Mom would feel guilty about making me go back with her. I'd get to stay down home for the summer, maybe even longer. No more of that sweltering garden apartment with its gossipy courtyard and fishbowl living. No more leering, taunting looks from Alex Kirby or grimly menacing stares from his brother, Ace.

Pop's hand has left off smoothing my hair. He blinks rapidly and glances toward my mother's sleeping form. She hasn't stirred.

"Really," I assure him, "I'd like to stay here with you and Neil." Instinctively I lower my voice. "It's awful up there when there's no school. Hot and steamy and nothing to do. Mom's working out all the time, or running, or teaching those classes. I don't really have any friends. There's just this one freaky girl who moved into the court last week and . . . and she's not staying. The other people, I can't stand. Can't stand them at all . . ."

My voice has been gaining pitch. Pop clamps two fingers over my lips.

"Whoa," he says huskily, turning to check whether Mom's still asleep. "Stop a minute now and listen. It isn't that I wouldn't like to have you home, Marleen baby. I'd like nothing better than to have you and your mom both home." He's speaking quietly, so quietly I've got to lean forward to hear him. "But let's think this thing out a little. Did you talk to your mom about it?"

I nod vehemently. "Yes I did. On the drive down. She knows I hate it up there. I definitely mentioned I might want to move back here for the summer. I think

33

I could really be a help with the business and all. You could take more time off to go fishing. Remember how much you used to like to go fishing?"

Pop shrugs and heaves his heavy body around in the chair. I can tell this whole conversation is making him uncomfortable. "What about your mom? Did she say it was okay with her?"

"Well," I answer, trying to be honest, "we only batted it around a little bit. Then we got on some other subject. But, if you told her you needed me here, that I'd be working for you . . . well, I'm sure she'd understand."

A buzzing black beach fly has just started circling near Mom's neck and ear and, as I'm speaking, Pop and I are watching it tensely.

Pop brushes me aside and, picking up the newspaper, starts out of the chair. Maybe he can swat it away before it wakes her. "It wouldn't be exactly true," he murmurs, "about my needing you to work for me. The phone tape takes pretty good messages most of the time, and the billing is no big deal. I think we should talk it over with your mom, Marleen. Got to try to be fair."

I sit back on my knees, feeling dismay. He's afraid of Bobbie. I just know it. And I'm stuck. I'm the ball that belongs on her side of the court. He won't pick it up without her permission. I don't hate my mom, but look at what she's doing, dividing my loyalty this way.

Pop's still trying to flag the fly away, bending almost tenderly over Mom, when the whole scene erupts with high-pitched screaming and flying sand.

Neil and Yolanda are back. They're acting overexcited and crazy, punching each other, grabbing handfuls of sand, staggering, stumbling, falling down and

34

getting up, pulling at each other's hair. It's Neil's favorite way of "playing," which I've always hated. But Yolanda seems to love it. She's a perfect match for him, tough and wiry and fast. Even her ear-piercing screeches and Neil's hoarse falsetto laughter seem to blend in a way that's exactly right.

Mom's awake of course in an instant, alert and ready to spring like a runner waiting for the starting gun. And she's laughing too. By now there's sand everywhere. It's on Neil's and Yolanda's faces and in their hair, it's coating Mom's sticky, sweaty skin and Pop's shirt and trousers. Only I've managed to scuttle away, crablike, still in a sitting position.

Suddenly Neil sees me. "You're too clean!" he yells, and with perfect aim he kicks what feels like a bucket of sand directly into my face, into my open mouth, my nostrils, my eyes. I feel like I'm smothering and being stung to death all at the same time. I can't see for the grit and instant tears in my eyes. I can't even yell.

Roughly, someone grabs my right wrist and pulls me to my feet. I feel like my arm's just been yanked from its socket. "Everybody in the water!" shouts the shrill voice beside me. It's Yolanda. "Come on, sister," she urges with a prodding hand at the back of my neck. "Last one in's a rotten egg."

Suddenly, half-blind, I'm part of this crazy stampede toward the ocean. Mom's leading the way. Directly behind her is Neil and, dragging me now by the fingertips, is Yolanda. Pop, of course, being fully dressed, isn't going in.

The moment we hit the waves, I pull free of Yolanda's clawlike grip and strike off on my own, rinsing my mouth and eyes in the harsh salty water as best I can. I just want to get as far away from all of them as possible, beyond the breaking surf into the calm sea. I'm a good ocean swimmer. The water here feels warm and friendly and buoyant.

I roll over on my back and float, closing my eyes against the dazzling sky. I know that everything that just happened was supposed to be in the spirit of fun. Yet I have a bad—even an eerie—feeling about it.

I'm thinking of the way Neil kicked that sand in my face. And I could just kill him for it, because I don't think it was fun. I think it was mean. Neil always boasts that he treats his women rough. He says they like it. Well, maybe Yolanda does.

I'm thinking, too, that I don't like Yolanda very much at all. She's exactly the kind of "woman" who makes it bad for the rest of us. Why does she let Neil get away with being such an ape? It only encourages him.

And, lastly, I'm thinking about whether I really do want to spend the rest of the summer down here at the shore. Pop doesn't want me unless Mom practically leaves me on the doorstep. Neil doesn't want me except as a target for his showing off to his girlfriends. And, as for Yolanda, where does she get off calling me "sister"? I don't want to be her sister any more than I want to be Neil's right now.

I turn over on my stomach, take a deep breath, put my face in the water, and kick off into a dead-man's float. Why, I wonder, has life started to feel like some big, mean, roughhouse game in which I'm always "it"?

5

Sweat Parties

THE SUNDAY NIGHT that Mom and I drove back from the Jersey shore, there was a ferocious thunderstorm. We didn't get home until nearly 2 A.M. The court lay in rain-washed silence and a gentle cooling breeze sprang up as we walked from the parking lot to the apartment.

How innocent the vacant stoops and darkened, sleeping windows looked. What evil could there be here that made me hate this place so? I glanced down one of the long arms of the buildings at the upstairs windows of the Kirby apartment, and they seemed harmless too. Maybe, as Mom said, it was just my teenage self-consciousness. Maybe I'd made up most of the horrors in my head.

Tired as she was from battling the pelting rain mile after mile, with very little help from our blurry old windshield wipers, Mom straightened her back and took a deep breath as she marched up the stoop. Once in the apartment, we threw open all the windows and the outdoor coolness swept in. Mom turned to me, her eyes glistening.

"You know, baby, that storm really helped clear the air. Since this weekend, I feel tremendously better about everything, don't you?"

I stood gazing at her, puzzled as to what she really meant. I knew that she and Pop had done some talking on Sunday morning over a late breakfast, most of which I'd slept past. Neil wasn't around, having left early for his job at the beach.

"Well, it's cooler anyway," I agreed.

Suddenly Mom's arms were around me. I couldn't see her face. But her voice sounded choked and husky in my ear. "I love you, baby," she whispered heavily, rocking me softly. "We both love you. Please remember that. And listen, it's going to be a really great summer for you. I've got plans, Marleen honey. So just give me this one chance, huh? You'll see."

She released her grip and left me standing there, staggering. I looked at Mom's face and saw that her cheeks were wet. For once I was sure the wetness wasn't sweat. It was tears.

"I . . ." I began, "I don't know what you mean."

Mom threw one arm loosely around my shoulder and we bumped our way along the narrow corridor to my bedroom. She had regained control of herself amazingly fast. Standing in the doorway of my room, she clapped her hands together briskly. The claps were like shots. They would have brought an entire gymnasium to attention.

"We're both too beat to talk anymore tonight," she replied. "Get to bed right away and sleep fast. Big week ahead. Chop-chop!"

Mom shut the door and I sank down on the bed, too exhausted to even take off my clothes. What was Mom trying to tell me? Was everything going to be great from now on because she'd won another round, convinced Pop that her "arrangement" was working out fine for everybody and was going to continue for a while? Or had she noticed how quickly I'd given up my idea of staying down at the shore with Pop and Neil, and was she feeling a little sorry for me?

I lay back and closed my eyes, too tired to think and glad to be home, wherever *that* was. It must have been in the very next instant that I fell fast asleep.

It's three days later and all at once our living room, which Rosalie admired so much because of its bare, uncluttered look, is filled from floor to ceiling with cartons and boxes. The place looks like a stock room, maybe even a warehouse. What's going on here?

What's going on is that Mom is taking on a new business. Let's call it a sideline. She's going to be a distributor for women's and children's "sweatwear"—warm-up suits, jogging outfits, running shorts, leotards, sneakers, sweat socks, headbands—you name it.

This new business is the brainchild of someone she met through the health club. And the way the stuff gets sold is through parties at people's houses or at their clubs or other organizations.

It's pretty clear to me, ever since yesterday when the stuff was delivered, that this is Mom's big plan for the summer and somehow for me. I'm going to be her assistant, checking stock, keeping records, accompanying her to the sweat parties, maybe even modeling some of the merchandise. Did she get this idea from my suggestion to Pop that I might help *him* out over the summer, which he must have told her about?

I can just see them, their heads together over the

breakfast table, Mom with her carob and yogurt waffles, Pop with his flapjacks and bacon, deciding that, "Yes, what Marleen really needs is something to keep her busy, make her feel important, take her mind off family and other 'things.' "

All Mom has told me so far is that she did discuss her new business venture with Pop. I suspect one reason was that she wanted his approval, and another was so he'd know that her little "experiment" in doing her own thing was far from over.

"Wah-hoo!" Suddenly there's a blood-curdling cry from one of the bedrooms and Rosalie comes crashing into the room. She takes a goofy stance, her knees bent and pointed outward, her head thrust forward and cocked to the side, and asks nearsightedly, "Tennis, anyone?"

Rosalie's been here for a couple of hours, helping me unpack cartons and fill in stock sheets. Now she's wearing an oversize yellow warm-up suit decorated with black stripes and oriental-looking insignia. The seat and the trouser legs are full and floppy. Even the ankle cuffs are loose, held up only by a pair of huge sneakers decorated with wide, colored stripes and arrows. She's removed her glasses and she's wearing a sharply peaked tennis cap with a deep visor. She looks like a cartoon character with the head of a duck.

I flop down on one of the unopened cartons and gaze at her, rolling my eyes to the ceiling.

"Not my style, eh?" she asks. "Is that what you're trying to say?"

"We-e-e-e-ll," I drawl. Then we both burst out laughing.

Rosalie sits down on a carton opposite me and pulls off the top of the warm-up suit. That and the other stuff she has on come, of course, from Mom's new sweatwear collection. Rosalie must be steaming inside that outfit. The hot weather has returned and the apartment is back to its usual bake-oven temperature.

Underneath all this junk she's just tried on, Rosalie is wearing her "usual" clothes. Today she has on what appears to be a man's deep-cut underwear shirt, trimmed with sequins if you can believe it, and a pair of filmy red Turkish trousers that look like they once belonged to a belly dancer. I haven't asked her yet where she gets her clothes. I'm still working up the courage.

She dashed up here this afternoon, pushing herself into the living room as usual, no questions asked.

"What gives?" she demanded. "Yesterday I watched this truck unloading, from the back window of my apartment. Then I went to the front window and saw they were taking all the stuff up to your place. You moving in or out?"

"Neither," I replied. And then I told her about the sweat parties.

"Great idea," she remarked, walking around and surveying the cartons like some kind of an expert, her hands planted on her hips. "Everyone's on a fitness craze these days. Nobody even wears regular clothes anymore. It's all sweat shirts and running pants. Your mom could make a bundle if she's good at this party stuff and knows enough people. After all, they sell pots and pans and plastics and makeup and even lacy, black underwear at house parties, so why not this stuff?"

Rosalie seems very savvy about a wide variety of subjects. And until I know her better maybe I shouldn't question her judgment. Besides, her words make me feel a lot more enthusiastic about this new part-time business Mom's plunging into.

The next thing that happens is that Rosalie's helping me unpack the cartons and check what's inside against the packing lists, the way Mom told me to. Rosalie helps me shift things around, classify the different kinds of merchandise, and organize them by style, color, and size. She's quick and smart, and what seems like a mountain of work goes surprisingly fast.

One of the reasons I'm in such a hurry to make sense out of this "sweatwear jungle," as Rosalie calls it, is that the very first sweat party is tonight. It's going to be at the home of one of Mom's body-building pupils, a rich Westchester lady with a large house that is, fortunately, air-conditioned.

When Mom rolls in around five o'clock after teaching her last class of the day, Rosalie and I have everything ready that has to go downstairs into the car trunk—boxes filled with samples of sizes, styles, and colors; order sheets for the customers who'll be at the party; and a big fat order book.

Rosalie and Mom haven't met yet, so I make a quick introduction.

Rosalie lurches forward in her Turkish belly-dancer trousers and gives Mom a hearty handshake. "So you're Bobbie. Glad to make your acquaintance. I hear you're a very unique woman."

I can see Mom's dark eyes flicker with surprise at the words and appearance of this strange, pudgy-faced pygmy in freaky clothes and dark sunglasses. I've never had a friend like this, *if* that's what Rosalie is. Over Rosalie's head, I signal to Mom with a hunch of my shoulders, trying to remind her that I *told* her this new kid in the court was weird.

"Unique?" Mom repeats with a questioning sigh. "Well, I don't know exactly what that's supposed to mean." She glances in my direction. She's no doubt wondering how come Rosalie has called her Bobbie, and also what else I've been saying about her to someone who's practically a stranger.

All I can do is toss out another shoulder hunch. Fortunately Mom doesn't pursue the subject.

"I'm beat," she says. She does look worn out. I think she's nervous about tonight. "And," she reminds me, "we have to leave here around seven, Marleen. So show me what you've got done, and then I'm going to do some yoga and meditation to relax."

Listening to my explanation—with lots of help from Rosalie—of how we've set things up, Mom appears pleased.

"Fine," she says, giving me the key to the car trunk. "You two can go on down and load this stuff that's going. And try to keep the noise around here at a minimum for the next half hour, hmmm?"

She heads for her bedroom where she keeps a big mat stretched out on the floor for her yoga exercises.

Rosalie shakes her head with admiration. "Great woman, your mom. She's really with it, you know. My parents are okay but they're . . . well, boring. Very ordinary. I like people who are different. With a style of their own."

I sigh. "You wouldn't like it too much when people make fun of your mom behind her back because she's such a . . . a jock and a muscle-building nut and all. *She* doesn't care. But I do."

"Oh, baloney," Rosalie snaps. "Why should you? Don't be such a milksop. Look at me. *I'm* weird. Think *I* care?"

43

All this time Rosalie is filling my outstretched arms with boxes, one on top of the other, and pretty soon we're on our way downstairs, she first and me following carefully behind.

Sure enough Mrs. Hofmeier is still sitting out. I don't think she has her supper until after dark these summer evenings, so as not to miss anything that might be going on in the court.

"Hi ho," Rosalie calls to her merrily, lifting two fingers in the air as we go dashing by on our way to the parking lot.

Mrs. Hofmeier looks too startled to say anything. Her pale eyes practically pop at the sight of tall, skinny me, cardboard boxes piled to my chin, and swift-moving Rosalie in baggy semi-sheer trousers, carrying the heavy order forms and order book and dangling Mom's car keys from her pinky.

As we round the corner of the building and disappear from Mrs. Hofmeier's line of vision into the parking lot, Rosalie chuckles. "See, that's the technique. Always attack first and leave 'em speechless. Stick around me, kid, and you'll learn how to enjoy being different."

I nod, moving my head as little as possible, and point Rosalie toward Mom's car with my eyes. She puts down the stuff she's carrying and starts fiddling with the trunk lock.

Too late, I remember that it's slightly broken and tricky to open. Rosalie jiggles the key this way and that. "Maybe I've got it in upside down," she mutters. "It seems stuck. Now I can't get it in or out."

All this time I'm standing there, hopping from one foot to the other. I can't put the boxes down. They're

44

practically wedged between my aching arms and the underside of my chin.

"T . . . take some of these things off the top," I urge her, "so I can get rid of the rest of them. And let me try."

"No, wait," Rosalie hisses, her ear close to the lock, like a safecracker waiting for the tumblers to fall into place. "I just heard something go 'click.' Or maybe it broke for good. I'm not sure."

"Rosalie!" I squeal. My patience is wearing thin. Sweat's running off my forehead and onto my cheeks and chin. I can actually cast my eyes down onto the topmost box and see dark droplets forming there. "Will you *please* take these things . . ."

Even before I've finished speaking, there's a harsh, guffawing noise directly behind my ear. It's a cross between the bray of a donkey and a horse laugh. It actually sends chills down my spine, and I give such a sudden start that the boxes I'm holding rise in a tower of gray cardboard, break free of my grasp, and seem to heave skyward.

The next moment they begin slipping off each other sideways and start crashing to the ground. The covers come off, spilling brightly colored leotards and tee-shirts and running shorts all over the oil-stained pavement of the parking lot.

"For crying out loud," says the owner of the guffawing voice. He's standing directly in front of me now, surveying the damage at my feet and scratching his thick, dirty-gold hair.

It's Alex Kirby and, as I watch a smirk spread slowly across his suntanned, crooked-featured face, he fixes me with an innocent stare and says, "Did *I* make you do that?"

45

6

Alex Kirby

IN A FLASH, Rosalie and I are down on the ground scrambling to retrieve the spilled sweat clothes and get them back in their boxes. We're so frantic that, as we both reach for the same half-emptied box, we smack foreheads hard. I actually see stars and sit back on my heels to clamp a damp palm to the spot, wondering if I'm going to raise a bump.

Alex Kirby finds this excruciatingly funny. His laughter rings across the parking lot and bounces off the backs of the buildings. He squats down in his skinny-legged jeans to examine the scene better. Out of the corner of my eye I can see his knee and one of his hands dangling loosely, the wrist resting on his kneecap.

"Boy, are you two dames FUN-NY," he exclaims between choking fits of laughter. "Anyone ever tell you you oughtta be on TV?" He shoots a finger at Rosalie. "What's she dressed up for? Halloween ain't for three months yet."

Rosalie gives him a long, hard look and draws herself up to her full standing height, which isn't much.

"You . . . turkey," she says vehemently. "If you're not going to help clean up, why don't you just shove off. This is no sideshow. So get lost."

"Sez you, it ain't." Alex scratches behind his ear and looks at me with a puzzled grin. "Can't figure out where all these weirdos are coming from lately." He leans forward and I can see that his skin is spotty under his tan. "Tell me something, kid. Is that strong dame with the red hair and all the muscles *really* your old lady?"

I flare up with anger and jump to my feet. One foot kicks out at him in a knee-jerk reaction, but falls far short of the mark.

"Oh my," Alex says in a falsetto voice, mockingly raising one hand to shield his face. "This one's a real terror. Bet you could beat me to a pulp." He swivels toward Rosalie, still squatting. "Or," he says, reaching into his tee-shirt pocket for a cigarette, "are you the one who's gonna lay me out?"

Rosalie levels a long look at him. "Get up," she says in a commanding voice.

Obediently Alex slowly rises to his full height. At fifteen he's already nearly six feet tall. He towers over Rosalie. They look ridiculous standing face to face.

"Now," Rosalie says, "you can hit *me* if you want to. Go on, try it, you dodo. I'm waiting."

Alex looks at her with a mixture of contempt and indifference. He takes a lighter from his jeans pocket and flicks the cap. Nothing happens. Alex flicks it again with his thumbnail, more sharply this time. Still no light.

Rosalie stands her ground and sends me a sly look of amusement.

Alex makes one last desperate try with the lighter. A weak flame springs forth and he buries the end of his cigarette in it. It's pretty clear he's not a practiced smoker. But he does manage to take a strong enough puff to keep the cigarette glowing. Then he lowers his head, slowly opens his mouth, and blows smoke directly into Rosalie's face.

"Creep!" she screams at him. "Coward! Lunk-head!"

Alex has already begun to stroll away from us, figuring he's scored the final point. But Rosalie's cries stop him in his tracks. He turns around menacingly and starts back toward us. I'm frozen with loathing. Rosalie is flaming mad. There's a yellow light in Alex's eyes. Maybe it's just the late-day sun slanting across the backs of the buildings.

Alex draws his lips back and bares his teeth at us. "Ah-h-h," he growls in utter disgust. With that he kicks hard at the rear bumper of Mom's car. And the very next moment the trunk lid flies open! Alex slouches away, and Rosalie and I stare at each other in shock and amazement.

We wait until he's completely out of sight and then we hastily get to work putting the boxes in order and stowing them in Mom's car trunk. Even Rosalie seems to have run out of things to say. When we've finished, we close the trunk and it locks fine. I try the key again just to make sure, and the trunk opens and closes with no trouble. In some crazy way, Alex's kick must have set things right.

We start back for the apartment. "I hope he broke

all six toes," Rosalie remarks. "Don't tell me that retard really lives in the court."

"It's all too true," I assure her. "In fact, he lives a couple of apartments down the line from you, in the opposite wing."

"A totally putrid character," Rosalie pronounces. "And a pea-brain, for sure. What did he mean about your mother?"

"Oh, that," I say with a shudder. And I proceed to tell Rosalie about Mom's having stopped to help push the Kirby brothers' car. "It was the meanest trick of fate," I mutter. "Because I clearly saw the two of them snickering and making fun of her only a couple of days before it happened."

"Bad luck," Rosalie comments.

"It's my mother's fault," I say, whispering now because we're mounting the steps to the apartment. By some miracle, Mrs. Hofmeier has vanished and the stoops and benches of the court are deserted. "She never should have stopped to help. But no, she has to be such a do-gooder. And also she *is* a sort of show-off. You know, she feels she has to prove women can handle heavy jobs as well as men."

"Well, in her case she can," Rosalie retorts. "Don't put the blame on your mother, Marleen. That kid and his brother are just a pair of goons, insecure males who can't stand to be threatened by a woman. It's not her problem; it's theirs."

"It's mine, too," I say, my voice rising. "How'm I supposed to deal with it?"

Rosalie shrugs her bare shoulders. "Ignore 'em. What else?"

"I can't," I say, feeling fresh flashes of anger licking

like flames at my insides. "I . . . I want to get back at them. I want to get even."

Rosalie stares at me, her dark glasses very still. We've reached the topmost stair, but I haven't opened the door to the apartment yet. "What do you have in mind?" she asks softly.

"I . . . I don't know," I stammer. "I wish I could call on . . . on all the forces of evil in the world. I wish I could think of something straight out of . . . of the worst horror movies and . . . and have it happen to Alex Kirby."

Rosalie smiles faintly. Her mouth, lips serenely drawn back across her teeth, has an almost sinister look. "You're serious, aren't you?"

"I think I hate boys," I say. "They all seem so . . . nasty. What have they got against us anyway?" I'm thinking partly of my brother Neil as I say this, and also of how only a short time back I used to look out across the court and wish that Alex Kirby would notice me.

Now he's noticed me, all right, and I'm just some dumb-looking, skinny, thirteen-year-old girl with a freaky mother for him to jeer at. I hate him worse than poison. I hate myself for ever having thought he was . . . somebody I'd like to know.

Rosalie is watching me closely. She doesn't know anything about the way I used to watch Alex Kirby all those months before she moved into the court. And she doesn't know anything about my brother Neil or the way I've been feeling about the way he treats me. She puts her small curved hand on my wrist. Her fingers are surprisingly cool. Even cold. "We'll go to another horror movie real soon," she says in a level voice. "Yes?"

Her words are almost mesmerizing. "Yes," I respond automatically.

"It'll be a lot bloodier and scarier than the last one," she promises. "Think you'll be able to take it?"

I nod like a sleepwalker.

"Okay," Rosalie whispers eerily. "I'll come around tomorrow. In the morning. So we can make plans." She starts down the stairs. "Got to run now," she says in a more normal voice. She turns. "Oh and, by the way, have a great sweat party this evening. Hope you sell out half the stock."

My mind is so full of what we've just been talking about that I've completely forgotten about the sweat party. "Um, thanks," I say, startled, as she flies down the rest of the steps.

Slowly I turn the knob and open the door into the living room. It's very silent in the apartment. Mom should be finishing up her meditation pretty soon now though. Then we'll have a quick supper of nut-and-vegetable cutlets or something like that and be off into the Westchester hills. But the evening ahead just doesn't hold any reality for me. Only one thing does.

"Alex Kirby," I whisper to myself determinedly under my breath. "Alex Kirby is going to get *his*."

7

The Gentle Pause

THE SWEAT PARTY was a success, and so was Bobbie. At first I felt shy and left out of things. Even though Mom had introduced me, I don't think most people knew who I was. Somehow Bobbie and I just didn't "go" together. But there was nothing new in that.

It wasn't until the room had filled up with people that Angie Horton, the woman who had offered her house, came and put her arm around my waist. She was shorter than I was and not at all brawny, but she was well-knit and perfectly trim. Her arm felt like a circlet of steel.

"I'm so glad to meet you, Marleen. I think it's going to be a great party, don't you?"

I nodded. Her manner was confidential and earnest, as though she really cared.

"Your mother says you've been an enormous help getting everything ready on such short notice." She paused, waiting, I guess, for me to say something. But I couldn't think of anything to say. "You must know," she went on, "how much we all think of your mother over at the health club." Her surprisingly soft brown eyes sought mine. "Well, believe me, she's terrific!"

With her final words, Mrs. Horton added an emphatic squeeze of my waist and I nearly toppled over. Then she left.

I busied myself laying out the merchandise Mom was going to display on the long table set up in front of the fireplace. The brightly colored sweat clothes looked out of place in Angie Horton's living room. It was high-ceilinged, paneled in dark wood, and trimmed with stone, like a room in a medieval castle. It made me think of dread deeds like daggers slashing through the thick draperies, of trap doors and bloody screams—a good setting for a horror movie.

Instead there were all these outdoorsy-looking women of various ages, sizes, and shapes milling around, chattering noisily, drinking chilled tomato juice and eating chunks of raw vegetables smeared with tofu dip. Mom didn't know everybody, of course, but her "groupies" had really spread the word about her. And I could see she was pleased to be the center of attention at such a good turnout. I suppose she felt like a celebrity.

Then everything got quiet and she was "on." She started her sales pitch and I could tell she was nervous at first. But as soon as she got into the comparative merits of the quality items she was selling and the poorer grades they sold in the stores, her zeal began to run away with her. And everybody listened carefully because, after all, she was a sports authority who had won medals and trophies.

Later, when we started writing up orders, I caught some of the enthusiasm, too, especially when Mom referred people to me because I was the expert on the sizes and colors that were available in the different models.

By the time we got home, it was after eleven. In the excitement of the last part of the evening, I had almost forgotten the court and the scene earlier that day with Alex Kirby. But everything came flooding back to me as we parked the car in the rear lot. Mom had pulled up alongside this maroon heap that looked almost exactly like ours and, in an instant, I realized it was Alex's brother's car.

"What are you staring at?" Mom wanted to know, as I got out and went over to peer inside the Kirby car.

I didn't answer because I didn't really know. And then, for some reason that wasn't at all clear to me, I tried the door handle. The car wasn't even locked.

"Marleen," Mom said sharply. "What are you doing there? Come and help me with these boxes." After the party, we had dumped all the remaining sweatwear samples and the order forms in the back seat.

"It's not even locked," I murmured as I slammed the rusty, creaking car door shut.

"So what?" Mom snapped. "Do you go around trying car doors for kicks or something? I honestly don't understand you, baby."

I looked at Mom. "Don't you even know whose car this is? It's the Kirby boys' car. It's the very car you pushed that day for those two . . . punks."

Mom sighed wearily. "Oh those two. Well, what difference does it make? I've told you before, I wish you'd forget about them, Marleen."

"It's not that easy," I replied. "That creep, Alex Kirby, came in the parking lot this afternoon when Rosalie and I were loading your car."

"And?"

"And . . . well, we had a . . . a fight."

Mom stopped unloading boxes onto the pavement. "He hit you?"

"No," I said hastily. "Nothing like that. Although I wouldn't put it past him. It was mostly, well, name-calling. And then he kicked the . . . the bumper of your car. Hard. So hard the trunk flew open."

Mom stared at me for a moment. And then she broke out into a hoarse, throaty laugh, a laugh of really deep-down enjoyment.

"You think it's funny?" I demanded.

"Ye-e-e-s," Mom gurgled between bursts of laughter. "I think it's funny. It also happens to be a very good way of getting that trunk to open when the latch sticks. You should have thanked him."

"Thanked him!" I exclaimed, thoroughly outraged. *"Thanked* him!" It was just no use trying to get Mom to understand anything about my feelings. Even if I'd told her that Alex had referred to her as "that strong dame with the red hair and all the muscles," she wouldn't have cared.

Without another word, I picked up my half of the stuff from the pavement and began following Mom into the court. "Pay him *back,"* I muttered softly to myself. "Pay him *back* is a lot more like it."

Where is Rosalie? I got up early this morning to work on completing the sweatwear order forms from last night. I wanted to be ready to leave whenever she came to call for me. I've heard of these all-day horror movie festivals. Maybe we could find one playing somewhere.

Now it's nearly lunchtime. I've been jumping up every few minutes to look out the window. It's overcast and sultry out, and there aren't many people around. Even Mrs. Hofmeier went in early today for lunch. I've been fantasizing all morning about a really juicy, bloody, scary movie. No matter what happens, I won't cringe. I won't pinch Rosalie until she's black and blue, I'll just picture Alex Kirby as the victim— Alex Kirby and the axe murderer, Alex Kirby and the chain-saw gang, Alex Kirby and the slimy blob from outer space!

At last, Rosalie is dawdling up the walk toward my stoop. Of all things, she looks almost normal today— baggy jeans and a sleeveless turtleneck. It's a terrible choice for her figure, of course. She looks dumpy and hippy in those jeans and how can she stand a turtleneck in this weather?

I open the door and watch her slowly mounting the stairs to the apartment. She's in no hurry.

"Don't rush," I say sarcastically. "I've only been waiting a couple of hours."

Rosalie shoves past me without a word and flops into a chair. That's her way. She always walks in here like she owns the place.

"Don't get pushy," she warns, fixing me with a Mafia-like stare of her dark glasses. "I've had a rough morning with my mother."

I sit down opposite her. Rosalie never talks about her family. All I know so far is that she thinks her parents are boring and that she's got an older sister who's "gorgeous" and is a counselor at a tennis camp in New England.

"Oh," I say, contrite. "What's the problem?" It's nice to know that somebody else is having mother troubles, too, even though hers are probably very different from mine.

Rosalie draws her feet up under her onto the seat of the chair. It's amazing that somebody with such short legs has that much dexterity. She looks like an unsmiling Buddha. Her hair is pushed up off her neck and piled on top of her head today and her pale lips are grim.

"It's all pretty revolting," she says, "a perfect example of the masses triumphing over the individual, of the herd trampling the human soul."

I squint. What is she going on about?

"Oh, why am I telling this to you?" she says. "You're just like the rest of them."

"Rosalie," I say irritably. "What have *I* got to do with it? I don't even know what you're talking about. Yet."

"All right," she says. "I'll tell you what she did. She threw away my see-through Turkish trousers. *Threw* them away. They went out with the garbage last night and were picked up and compacted by heavy machinery while I slept. Gone." Rosalie folds her arms across her chest indignantly. "Finished. Forever!"

"Oh," I say, after a pause. *"Those* trousers, huh? The ones you wore yesterday."

"What others?" she says miserably. "They were all I had. They once belonged to a real belly dancer. She got too fat for them and had to give them away. I treasured those pants. I really did."

I try to nod sympathetically. Rosalie seems very broken up about this. "They were awfully filmy, though," I remark cautiously. "I guess your mother didn't think they were . . . proper."

"Pooh," Rosalie exclaims. "I was wearing panties

57

underneath. If I'd had on a pair of running shorts, you'd have seen a whole lot more, and nobody would have said a word. People are such hypocrites."

I sit up, startled. "Did somebody say something?"

"Of course," Rosalie replies. "Weren't you listening? What did you think I meant about the trampling herd? Mrs. Hofmeier and her biddy friends were sitting out last night. My mom went over to chat with them and Mrs. H remarked on my 'costume.' She said it might give certain 'young men' in the court the wrong idea about me. 'Young men!' Maybe she saw that tangle we had in the parking lot with Alex Kirby. She *could* have watched from her back window. If you remember, she wasn't on her stoop anymore when we went back to the apartment. She had probably gone inside right after we passed, so she could spy on us."

I utter a deep breath of recognition. "So-o-o-o," I say.

"So," Rosalie responds abruptly.

"And *she* thought you were leading Alex Kirby on with your see-through trousers," I sputter.

Rosalie laughs too. But bitterly. "Yeah. That clunk. Nauseous-making, isn't it?"

I get up and go to the window. I can't think of anything else to say on the subject of Rosalie's trousers. And Mrs. Hofmeier's suspicious mind just makes me sick. I've got to get Rosalie onto other things.

"Well," I remark, "if we're going to that horror movie you promised me, why don't we leave right this minute? Mrs. Hofmeier is still inside having her lunch or whatever. It's probably a good time to escape."

But Rosalie doesn't budge. "How was the sweat party?" she says. "I should have asked sooner."

"Great for my mom," I say, pointing to the order

58

forms I've been working on. "But I'll tell you about it on the way. What movie did you pick?"

Rosalie still hasn't moved from her Buddhalike pose on the chair. "No movie," she says.

"No movie!" I say with dismay. "Why?"

"No money," she replies. "No allowance, no traipsing around, no nothing. I'm docked."

"But why?"

"Because," she says impatiently, "I was 'fresh,' I was 'nasty,' and I wasn't supposed to wear those trousers outside the house in the first place. So all I'm allowed to do for the next two weeks is to go and work at THE GENTLE PAUSE."

"The gentle *what?*"

"Paws. Paws," Rosalie repeats, getting up on her knees, sticking out her tongue, and letting her hands hang limply from her wrists. "*Paws* like a doggie. Only not really. It's a play on words, see? So they spell it *p-a-u-s-e*, like 'stop and browse.' But it also means *paw*, like bow-wow and meow and stuff like that. Get it?"

I shake my head hopelessly. Maybe Rosalie has flipped altogether since the loss of her trousers.

She gets up from the chair at last and reaches delicately for my hand.

"Look, my dear," she says, "why don't I simply *take* you there and then you can see for yourself. It's a dusty, cobwebby old thrift shop that raises money for an animal charity. It's not too far a walk, down by the railway station. My mom volunteers there. Now and then they have some fascinating junk that people contribute. And occasionally great old clothes. Where do you think I got my Turkish trousers?"

Now, finally, everything is falling into place. Rosalie has been picking out her clothes at the thrift shop

59

where her mother works. There's always something weird in the piles of stuff people get rid of. And even nonweird stuff looks fairly weird on Rosalie. I have a hunch, too, that she's been using this dressing up as a way of getting back at her "ordinary" parents, and also her "gorgeous" sister at tennis camp.

"Hmmm," I murmur, taking a final look around as I prepare to leave the apartment with Rosalie. "THE GENTLE PAUSE. I like the name already. It even sounds a little spooky. Cobwebs. Old clothes and stuff. What else do they have there?"

8

By the Railway Tracks

THE RAILWAY STATION is a brisk walk on a cool, pleasant day. Today is not one of them, and we drag along, inhaling leaden, moisture-filled air. Occasionally a gust of wind, like the breath of a blast furnace, hits us. It's no relief.

"Is the . . . the shop air-conditioned?" I gasp hopefully.

Rosalie looks at me. "Air-conditioned? For Pete's sake, you must be hallucinating." She touches my arm apologetically. "Okay, okay. I know a horror movie would have cooled us off. But think of it this way. My mom has the car with her, so we'll surely get a lift home."

I trudge on in silence, a little sorry now that I've agreed to go to the thrift shop with Rosalie. Maybe I should have gone to a horror movie by myself. It's crazy, I know, but I can't stop having these thoughts of revenge.

Why should people get away with making me feel stupid? Neil, Yolanda, the Kirby boys, all those laughing passing strangers. Harmless, skinny Marleen, huh? The jock-lady's quiet, white-faced daughter, huh? Neil's "rotten-egg" sister who gets sand kicked in her face and then gets dragged half-blinded into the water by his shrieking girlfriend.

Doesn't anybody realize that I have feelings? Don't they understand that deep down inside me there's a screaming, insistent voice that keeps telling me I *must* get my own back?

How, though? I just don't know how. I've heard that some people believe you can get back at your enemies by making little images of them out of wax and then sticking pins into the tiny figures. Others think you can go to a witch or a fortune-teller and get a curse put on somebody. I wonder if anything like that would work. And what would it cost? How do you find such a person? Do you look up "witches" in the Yellow Pages?

"Watch out!"

Rosalie has grabbed me by the arm, her curving fingernails digging sharply into my flesh. Just as I was about to step off the curb, one foot already hanging in midair, a car has come screeching around the corner of the street. It passes so close to me that I can feel a scorching wind sweep past the tip of my nose.

I lurch back in shock. What color was that car? I could swear it was maroon, with rusted doors and two guys with dirty-blond hair and spotty suntanned faces in the front seat . . .

"You weren't looking," Rosalie scolds. "I'm sorry if I hurt you." She examines my arm. Sure enough there are three tiny semi-circular reddened cuts in the pale skin just above the elbow.

"Goons on wheels," Rosalie says. "You can't cross

streets that way, Marleen. Didn't your mother ever tell you?"

My mind is on one thing only. "It *was* who I thought it was, wasn't it?" I say, looking toward the empty street down which the speeding car has vanished.

"Was who? Was what?" Rosalie waves a hand in front of my eyes. "Are you in some kind of trance? Do you know those are the first words you've spoken in ten minutes? What's got you? Is it the heat?"

"That car, Rosalie," I insist. "Didn't you see what color it was?"

"Yeah. Green," she replies. "Or gray. Maybe it was brown with yellow polka dots. Who noticed? I was too busy saving your life."

"It was maroon," I say. "I'm sure it was. Alex Kirby and his brother were in that car. Don't you see?"

Rosalie starts us walking again. "Never," she says. "It wasn't maroon. And the guy at the wheel had black hair and he was alone."

"How can you be so sure?" I demand. "You just said it was green. Then you said gray. You admitted you didn't really notice."

Rosalie sniffs. "Well, I noticed that much. It might make a neat story, kiddo, but it just happens not to have been Alex Kirby. You're getting a fixation, you know that? A dangerous fixation."

Rosalie is maddening. Even if I was wrong about what I thought I saw (and I don't think I was), I'd have expected her to be much more understanding. Alex Kirby's begun to cause her trouble too. Can't she see how I feel?

Maybe it was the shock of what just happened, but I'm suddenly desperately thirsty, parched. I remember that I didn't have any lunch, not even a drink of water, before leaving home—and where *is* this GENTLE PAUSE anyway?

We're walking alongside the railroad trestle now. The high embankment with the tracks on top is on our left. On the right side of the road are patches of tall grass flattened here and there with rusting bedsprings, old refrigerators, and hulks of dumped machinery. There are no shops or stores anywhere in sight. Yet we must be getting near the railway station with its busy plaza and parking lot.

Suddenly Rosalie halts. "Here we are," she announces.

I look up. All I see is a funny little two-story house built out of gray stone. It has a brown shingle roof and an outside staircase of dark brown wood that connects the lower and upper parts. The entire building is nestled into the steep incline of the railway embankment. It looks a little like a miniature Swiss chalet that somebody put there a long time ago and forgot about.

"This is it?" I say with disbelief. I'd expected a real shop in a whole row of stores.

Rosalie nods. "Quaint, huh? It used to be the signalman's house, oh ages ago. See, he could bunk downstairs and then, when he needed to flag a train in or out, he'd go racing up the stairs to the second story, which was level with the tracks. Of course, all the signaling's been automated for a long time now. The building was left vacant for years."

I nod. "It still looks . . . well, peculiar."

"Don't knock it," Rosalie replies. "The house was so bad a few years ago that it was condemned. It was full of rotted timbers and infested with rats. Then this charity outfit started looking for a place for a thrift shop, and they got the town to fix it up a little and give it to them rent-free."

Sure enough I notice that a small parking lot has been bulldozed out of the embankment on the far side of the building and there are a couple of cars parked in it.

"It's a neat idea," I agree. "But how does anybody ever find the place? It seems to be in the middle of nowhere."

"Ah," Rosalie answers, "it only looks like that. Don't you know where we are? We're practically around the corner from the station plaza. And there's a big sign there with an arrow." She leans a little closer. "I brought you here by my secret back road." Then, drawing her lips across her teeth in her special horror movie leer, she whispers in a phony Count Dracula accent. "You don't know very much about vot goes on in dis town, do you, little vun?"

Inside THE GENTLE PAUSE we're greeted by a large, imposing woman who seems to be wearing a stethoscope around her neck. On closer inspection, I see that it's a piece of silvery metal jewelry. The neckpiece is a thick curved rod. All sorts of huge clanking objects are suspended from the lower part of the necklace, as if from a giant charm bracelet.

"Ah, Rosalie," the woman says warmly, "your mother's been expecting you. She just popped out for a while to do some shopping."

Rosalie introduces me. The woman's name is Mrs. Bigelow, and she's one of the volunteer workers at the thrift shop. I didn't *think* she was Rosalie's mother, of course. Even though I only met Rosalie's mother once, I remembered she was small and sensible-looking and not at all the type to wear bizarre tin jewelry around her neck.

The shop is dimly lit and cluttered. There are racks of clothing, piles of books, and heaps of bric-a-brac. There's old furniture, too, some pieces sitting one on top of the other. And there are boxes of discarded jewelry—tangled chains and bracelets, earrings without mates, and fancy brooches with absent stones, like big front teeth that are missing.

Mrs. Bigelow glances around her helplessly. "Our trouble is," she remarks, looking at me with soulful, dark eyes, "that we have become a dumping ground. People bring us more than we can handle. There's no way to dig through and tag all this junk. We just don't have enough help."

Rosalie stands by nodding. "Summer's the worst time around here," she explains. "It's because of people doing spring cleanouts and bringing all their stuff to us. We can't sell much of it because, as the weather gets warmer, shoppers stop coming. Before Christmas is the best time. People'll buy anything then."

I look at the two sad faces and think of how much Rosalie helped me with the sweatwear stock just yesterday. I figure I owe her one.

"Well," I say, clearing my throat which seems to be full of dust, "I'm willing to stay and work this afternoon. I would like to get something to drink first, though."

Mrs. Bigelow jumps to attention and takes me into a little back room where there's a scarred, waist-high refrigerator that's chugging away noisily. Another donation, no doubt.

Rosalie joins me and we raid it for cold drinks, fruit, and a big bag of corn chips.

"Please girls," Mrs. Bigelow pleads from the doorway as she's leaving the room, "put those corn chips back in the refrigerator when you've finished with them. You know our problem here, Rosalie."

I gaze questioningly at Rosalie but she only flashes a secretive look at Mrs. Bigelow's back.

We drink and munch in silence. When we return to the main room of the shop, Rosalie says to Mrs. Bigelow, "I'll just show Marleen upstairs. Then we'll come back down and start work."

Mrs. Bigelow is now seated at a small desk trimmed with fancy, chipped carvings. She's trying to extract a long strand of bulbous blue beads from a complicated knot of other jewelry. I notice that in contrast to her heavy chest and tall, full figure, her fingers are surprisingly fine and slender.

We dash out the front door of the shop and around to the sagging wooden staircase at the side of the building. "What did she mean?" I ask, as we mount the crooked steps, "when she said 'you know our problem'?"

"Oh that," Rosalie mutters. She's standing on the top landing now. There's a doorway here that leads into the atticlike upper story of the old signalman's hut. Rosalie points to the door with a curving forefinger. "It's because of what's in there."

I bound onto the landing and peer over Rosalie's shoulder at the battered wooden door. It has two tiny glass panes near the top but they're thick with dust and smear marks. I crane my neck but I can't see anything inside.

"Sometimes, when it's real quiet in the shop," Rosalie explains softly, "you can hear them gnawing and scratching over our heads. Mrs. B's scared to death they'll get into the shop itself, especially if we leave food around. You see, there's a trap door in the ceiling. She's sure they're going to come crawling through it one of these days. Then—*whammo*— they land on our necks and shoulders, dig their claws in, and start working away on *us* with their teeth!"

Rosalie is doing her horror *schtick* again, her lips drawn back and her dark glasses impassive and sinister. She's definitely enjoying herself.

"Who," I ask, wishing I weren't so close to guessing the answer, "are 'they'?"

Rosalie doesn't give me a direct reply. Instead, she curls her own fingers into little claws and starts scratching on the door, all the while making sharp, squeaky noises.

"Did you know," she says, turning to me at last, "that rodents have front teeth that keep on growing from their roots, just like our fingernails? That's because they keep wearing away the tips with all that gnawing and gnashing. Nature's clever, huh?"

"Rats!" I exclaim, quickly backing down two steps from the landing. "Only I thought you said they got rid of them when they fixed up the building."

Rosalie hunches her shoulders. "*Maybe* they did. But listen, sweetie, a rodent's a rodent. Maybe it's only mice. Maybe it's squirrels. You think just because they have those darling bushy tails they aren't rodents? Take away the fluff in back and what have you got? A rat."

Rosalie pauses, watching my face. "Yeah, this place is practically a horror movie, isn't it?"

68

Before I can think of anything to say, Rosalie turns away again. "Oh well," she says over her shoulder, "as long as you're here, come see the railroad tracks."

Without a word of warning, she leaps off the back of the second-story landing onto a flat place near the top of the embankment. I hop up onto the landing and am about to follow her. Then I make a terrible mistake. I look down.

There's a gap, a little less than three feet across but it's a deep wedge that goes down, down, down beneath and behind the staircase.

"Oops," she says, turning and extending her hand, "you shouldn't have looked."

"But I did," I say, feeling my insides swirl and dip. I have a quick vision of the awful mash in my stomach—sour red plums, green grapes, and corn chips awash in a fizzy lemon-lime drink. Yuck. I swallow hard.

"Oh come on," Rosalie urges me with impatience. "If I can make it with these stumps for legs, you can with those long stems of yours."

Except that my "long stems," as Rosalie calls them, feel like cooked spaghetti. But I give her my hand and make the jump anyway. She scrambles a few more steps up the embankment and I follow.

"Wow." I stand there mesmerized. We're practically on the track. The gleaming rails, catching a shaft of light from the glowering sun, seem to go shooting past us at fantastic speed. What happens, I think to myself, when a train comes through? This is a dangerous spot and not that hard to reach. Do the town officials think that just because they sawed off part of the wooden ramp leading from the signal hut to the tracks, kids won't be able to get up there?

Rosalie looks at me. She's reading my mind all right.

"Talk about your horror setups," she says slyly. "How's this for a setting?"

I nod slowly, thinking how it wouldn't be at all impossible to get somebody you hated up here, rope them to the tracks, and then just wait for the 5:43 to come roaring along and do its work. A long shudder goes through my body. I can clearly see Alex Kirby, all nearly six feet of him, neatly laid out, lashed to the rails, and in the distance the screeching hoot and hiss of an approaching train.

But of course I'm being ridiculous. Hallucinating again, I suppose, Rosalie would say. And anyhow, Alex Kirby isn't exactly your perfect example of a helpless railway-track victim.

I turn, facing back toward the wooden landing, and my eye fixes on the door that leads directly into the attic of THE GENTLE PAUSE. Another thought—a strangely comforting one—hits me.

I think about what Rosalie's been telling me, about what probably lies behind that door. And suddenly I've got a brand-new vision. This time it's rodents. Rodents gnawing and scratching, rodents with ever-growing fangs, rodents busily ruffling their fur. Rodents sinking their sharpened teeth into Alex Kirby's none-too-clean neck!

9

Duncan Donuts

"AHOY UP THERE. Hey!"

A crackly male voice breaks into my nightmarish fantasy. There is somebody standing at the bottom of the signal-hut steps. My first thought is the police. We've been seen on the embankment and we're guilty of criminal trespassing. Worse, they've been reading my mind with radar. The charge is evil intent, murder aforethought.

Even as I look down on the caller, I'm trembling slightly. But why? He isn't in uniform. He isn't even a grown man. In fact, he's just a kid, maybe fourteen or fifteen.

He has a large-ish head of frizzy light brown hair and a broad turned-up nose. Teeth like piano keys. Yet he's pleasant-looking, with clear brown eyes.

Rosalie and I glance questioningly at each other. She shrugs. She doesn't seem to know him either.

"What's your problem?" Rosalie calls down. She's always ready to take the uppity approach. Why does she assume it's *his* problem, or even that there is a problem?

But in a way she's right. He has a question.

"Where's the entrance to this place? Up there?"

"Depends," Rosalie replies teasingly, "on what you're here for."

By way of an answer, the kid steps aside for a moment. Then he lifts up a sort of wire-mesh box. It's big and bulky, a rectangle, and seems to be closed on all six sides.

Rosalie turns to me. "Oh-oh," she hisses. "More junk. See the kind of stuff they try to unload on us?"

She starts down the rickety steps in a hurry and I follow.

"If this is a donation," she says snappily to the kid on the way down, "we probably don't want it. You'll have to go inside and ask. But you could save yourself the trouble."

By now Rosalie's leading the way toward the main entrance of the shop. She stops just short of the doorway and remarks over her shoulder, "What *is* that thing, anyway?"

I'm standing beside the kid now, though I haven't said a word yet. He's taller than he looked from up above. In fact, he's a little taller than I am. He's still funny-looking. And yet he has a nice face. I can't figure that out.

"What *is* it?" he repeats with amused surprise, his voice breaking slightly. "Can't you tell?"

We both look at the box again. It's sitting on the ground. Now I see that it must have a door because one of the side panels looks different from all the others. But I can't figure out how it opens. I decide to give it a try anyway.

"Is it a . . . a . . . a chicken coop?" A second thought strikes me. "Or a . . . a rabbit hutch?"

The kid cocks his head encouragingly. "No. But you're getting warmer. Take another guess."

I shrug. I'm clean out of guesses. And Rosalie seems suddenly struck dumb.

"I'll give you a hint." The kid crouches down beside the box and slides up the panel that looked different from the others. It latches automatically and stays up.

"Aha!" I grin. "I thought so. That's the door."

"So what," Rosalie says in a flat voice.

"So this," says the kid. "Hang on a minute."

He gets to his feet and starts searching on the ground for something. In a few moments he comes back with a piece of rock.

"Now watch," he commands. He lightly tosses the rock in through the open door. The next instant— *wham!*—the raised panel slams down and snaps shut with a clang.

"Oh wow," I shout, clapping my hands. "It's a trap. An animal trap." I turn to Rosalie. "Pretty clever, huh?"

The kid smiles modestly. "I made it myself. You probably won't be able to figure out how the response mechanism for the door works. It's my own design. Actually, I'll probably patent it one of these days."

I can tell he's proud of his invention. "What can you catch with this kind of trap?" I ask.

The kid scratches his head. "Most any kind of small animal," he replies, "just as long as you set it up with the right kind of bait. I've been using it mainly for squirrels. Got some young raccoons last spring. A field mouse now and then."

Rosalie gives him a sharp look. "So you're a fur-trapper, huh? How many squirrels you figure it would take to make a fur coat for little me?"

The kid stares at Rosalie indignantly. "No fur-trapper, lady. I'm a naturalist."

"Naturalist!" Rosalie challenges. "Catching inno-cent beasties in your big cruel cage. That doesn't add up at all, mister."

The kid gives her a hard look. "Duncan. The name's Duncan."

"Okay," she says, "Mr. Duncan."

He shakes his head. "Duncan's my first name."

Rosalie's in a peppery mood. "Oh really," she re-torts. "So what's your second name? Donuts?"

Duncan doesn't think this is very funny and, hon-estly, neither do I. "If you like," he answers very calmly.

Duncan Donuts. What an idea.

"What *do* you do with the squirrels you catch?" I ask hastily, trying to keep peace between him and Rosalie.

"Release 'em," Duncan replies. "But far away. Where they can survive okay and won't dig up gar-dens, eat bulbs, chew away at attics. It's a business. Maybe you even got one of my circulars."

He pulls a crumpled sheet of paper out of his pocket and shows it to me. It's a home-made job, hand-lettered and run off on a copying machine:

SQUIRRELS AND OTHER PROPERTY PESTS
Humanely caught and far-released.
Phone for prices

Down at the bottom there's a number to call.

Rosalie grabs the sheet and stares at it. "Yeah," she mutters, half to herself. "We had squirrels like crazy around our last house. They even got into the chim-

ney. But we never got one of these announcements."
She looks up. "So what are you doing now, giving up
the business?"

Duncan looks surprised. "Not at all. What makes
you think so?"

"This." Rosalie kicks Duncan's wire-mesh trap
lightly with her toe. "You came to donate it to THE
GENTLE PAUSE, didn't you?"

"Nope," Duncan replies. "*I* never said that. That's
what you said."

They stare at each other for a while with stubborn
expressions on their faces.

Rosalie turns to me, but I can't help her. Duncan's
right. She's been acting like a wise guy and she's made
some kind of mistake, jumping to conclusions all over
the place.

We're standing there, Rosalie and I, still trying to
figure out what Duncan's doing here, when the door of
THE GENTLE PAUSE opens and out comes Mrs. Bigelow.

She must have succeeded in extracting the gigantic
blue beads from the tangle on her desk because she's
wearing them around her neck now, instead of the
silvery stethoscope.

"Ah," she says, smiling, "I thought I heard voices
out here."

Her eyes light fondly on Duncan and to our surprise,
she leans right across us and embraces him.

"So you've brought it," she says, releasing him and
glancing with a slight shudder at the wire-mesh trap on
the ground. "I guess you've already explained to the
girls what you've come to do. When do you want to
get started, dear? Right now?"

I break into a sweat in the dead, humid air, thinking

of how really stupid we've been and how Duncan's led us on in his quiet way. He's certainly given Rosalie enough rope to hang herself.

Because it turns out that Duncan is Mrs. Bigelow's nephew. And he's come here today to try to trap whatever's crawling around, scratching and squealing and terrifying his aunt, up in the attic of THE GENTLE PAUSE.

It's late afternoon and, just as Rosalie promised, we're being driven home from the thrift shop in her mother's car.

We're filthy from long hours of dusting, sorting old clothes, and washing and polishing the bric-a-brac to be put out for sale. But we're reveling in the cooling breeze of the air-conditioning as it wafts around the back seat.

Soon after Duncan got to work, Rosalie's mother returned from her shopping in town. And shortly after that, Mrs. Bigelow, too nervous to hang around, apologetically took off.

All afternoon, as Rosalie and I worked, we could hear Duncan coming and going, as he entered and left the attic by the door at the top of the outside staircase. Occasionally there were horrible thumps and bangs overhead. Then everything would get deathly quiet.

"Do you think we should go up and see what happened?" I whispered to Rosalie once or twice.

But she just shook her head and kept on working. After a while there were no more noises, and we learned that Duncan had returned the key to Rosalie's mother and left for the day. The wire-mesh trap was nowhere in sight.

Most of the afternoon, Rosalie's mother was busy

with customers. They came in in twos and threes and puttered around trying on clothes and jewelry, examining the furniture, and wondering aloud among themselves about whether any of it was worth refinishing.

I could tell that there was still some stiffness between Rosalie and her mother as a result of their big argument that morning. Mrs. Grant even seemed a little cooler toward me, I thought, than the last time I'd met her when she'd driven us to the horror movie and back. Did she think *I'd* encouraged Rosalie to go prancing around the court in her belly-dancer trousers?

It's a short auto ride from the thrift shop to home, and in no time at all we're back. As we pull into the parking lot, Mrs. Grant turns around and thanks me for helping. This time she sounds pleasant and friendly.

"It was really good of you to volunteer today, Marleen. We all appreciate it."

"Maybe," I suggest, "if my mother doesn't need me for . . . other things, I can do it again."

"We'd be delighted," she replies.

As we stroll toward the entrance to the court, Rosalie sidles up to me.

"Like tomorrow?" she murmurs with a sly wink.

"Maybe," I answer, playing it straight. "If I'm free. Why not?"

"So you can find out what Duncan Donuts found in the attic, eh?"

"Well, sure," I say. "Aren't you curious?"

"Sure," Rosalie replies. "But not as curious as you are."

I glance at her with a slight frown. What is she getting at anyway?

Rosalie halts. Then, unexpectedly, she reaches up, pulls me down by the shoulders, and plants a kiss on my forehead.

"It's all right," she says almost tenderly. "I give you my blessing. You make a nice couple."

At that moment, Mrs. Grant, who's been walking ahead of us, turns and calls out to Rosalie in a firm tone. "I'll want you right now, Rosalie, to help with getting dinner."

Rosalie gives me a quick look of woe and flits off.

I stand there, mildly shocked but smiling to myself. There's just one question that pops into my mind. How can I like a boy and let Rosalie keep on calling him by a really dumb name like Duncan Donuts?

10

Baby-Sitting

A COUPLE OF weeks have gone by and the summer is in full swing. I'm busy all the time and, not-so-strangely I guess, I'm enjoying it. I've actually had to draw a July-August calendar for myself, penciling in the things I've got to do each day.

There are Bobbie's sweat parties, of course—about two a week to go to. And in between there are the orders that have to be filled, the fresh stock to be logged in, the sales records to be kept—lots of paperwork, most of which I do in the early mornings while it's still cool.

Most afternoons I'm at THE GENTLE PAUSE with Rosalie. Her two weeks of "punishment," when she had to be there every day, are just about up. But we still go because we've made so much headway sorting and tagging stuff that it seems a shame to give it up now. Also, Rosalie's mother and Mrs. Bigelow have reported that sales are picking up. They think it has a lot to do with the improvements we've made in the display of merchandise.

79

And then there's Duncan. He turns up a lot too.

At first, I thought we wouldn't see him again after he finished his work in the attic. He set his trap for two days running, and all he caught were a couple of mice. Mrs. Bigelow was relieved but not completely. Duncan reported there were quite a few gnawed-away knotholes, loose slats, and other not-so-small openings in the attic of THE GENTLE PAUSE.

So, after letting the mice go some distance away, in the tall grass opposite the railway embankment, Duncan went to work sealing up the attic. He hammered away over our heads for two afternoons, and that seemed to be the end of that.

But a couple of days later, there he was again. This time he had a woodworking kit with him. Maybe his aunt, Mrs. Bigelow, had suggested it. Or maybe it was his own idea. Anyhow, he started coming around to reinforce and "touch up" some of the more beat-up pieces of furniture that people had donated in order to make them more salable.

Most days he worked outdoors on the shady side of the signalman's hut. Yesterday was one of those days, and whenever I thought Rosalie wasn't watching me, I peeked out the window. Duncan was a mystery to me. He was friendly, and yet there was always a polite distance between us that I didn't think belonged there.

Maybe Rosalie thought we'd "make a nice couple." But so far we weren't anything of the sort.

Sure enough, Rosalie caught me staring at him. She doesn't miss much. "Gotcha!" she exclaimed from behind, finger-jabbing me hard in the ribs.

I screeched and spun around quickly, hoping Duncan wouldn't hear me. Luckily there was nobody in the shop at the moment.

"So what's your latest opinion of our friend, Mr. Donuts?" Rosalie demanded. "Is he a nerd, or what? How can he resist your exquisiteness, your made-for-each-other-ness? *And,* if he isn't interested in you, what's he doing around here? Does he really care about hammering that rickety rocking chair together? Why isn't he out catching squirrels for relocation and making himself some dough, eh?"

I moved away from the window feeling my neck and arms go hot. I had a theory that Duncan did sort of like me. But part of the problem was Rosalie. He and she had gotten off to a bad start. I noticed that he usually gave her a wide berth. And, of course, I was usually with Rosalie.

My problem, I'd decided, was how to get away from Rosalie for a while. I had the feeling that Duncan was the patient sort. I'd have to try to be patient too. But, after all, a summer doesn't last forever.

Today is a good day for thinking. In the midst of my being so busy with the thrift shop and the sweat parties, my baby-sitting job has turned up again. Mrs. Willis phoned last night and asked if I could take care of Erica this afternoon, while she goes to get her hair cut over at the mall.

The Willises live two courts away from us in the same garden-apartment development. They've been out of town visiting relatives, which is why I haven't heard from them in a while. Even though I didn't like missing a day at the thrift shop, I said yes right away. I could certainly use the money.

Erica is a bright-eyed, chubby-cheeked two-year-old. There's a broiling sun today and not a breeze stirring. So, before Mrs. Willis left, we set up Erica's kiddie pool just outside their ground-floor apartment and put in a few inches of water. Erica's got her rubber ducks, her plastic watering can, and all her other water toys, and she's playing happily.

Pretty soon I've got my sneakers off and my feet in the kiddie pool. I'm wearing shorts so, while sitting on the rim, I can get my legs in, too. I trail my hands and wrists in the cool water. Even though it's sure to warm up quickly in this heat, wet feels better than dry.

The Willises' court is smaller than ours, and there always seem to be fewer people around. Mrs. Willis says the apartments aren't as large, and most of the people who live in them go to business. It's lovely and peaceful. I wish our court were more like this. I feel safely enclosed here in a world of heat and quiet, a world of baby gurgles and occasional remarks from Erica such as, "Duckie go for a sim in de water." I can think about Duncan to my heart's content.

It seems disloyal to want to get away from Rosalie. After all, she's the one who took me to THE GENTLE PAUSE. If not for her, I never would have met Duncan. But how will I ever find out the truth about whether he likes me? It's important to me. Because I'm so astonished that after all my boy-hating, my terrible feelings toward Neil and toward Alex Kirby, I could actually meet a boy who seems to be a real human being and not some kind of ape.

Erica is telling me something. "Want to dig in de dirt." She's lifting one pudgy leg after another out of the kiddie pool. There's a little patch of garden just beside us with loose, dry soil where Mrs. Willis lets her dig with her plastic shovel. I help her out, reach for a towel to dry her off, and set her down alongside the pool.

I remain sitting in the kiddie pool all by myself and resume thinking about Duncan. If I could somehow spirit him away from the thrift shop this afternoon, if he were here right now, what would we talk about? There are so many things I don't know about him, where he lives, where he goes to school. Is it possible that we go to the same school and that we just never noticed each other? Might I see him there in the fall?

I can almost hear his voice. It has that odd crackle in it. Sometimes it breaks, but in an attractive way. All this time, I'm keeping my eyes on Erica. I never take them off her when I'm in charge of her. And yet I can hear a voice in the near distance, a voice that sounds a little hoarse and deep but that *could* be Duncan's.

It's wishful thinking, of course. I know that. Yet, I turn around so sharply that my legs swish and a gush of water splashes out of the pool.

All along, my back has been to the rest of the courtyard and to the sun. Now I'm blinking directly into it and I'm aware of a tall figure, almost a silhouette, standing across from me on the other side of the pool. I have to arch my neck back to see who it is.

As my eyes travel upward, I realize there are two figures. The one nearest to me is a girl, about my age or maybe a little older. From what I can see against the glare, she has small, pouty features and long, straight taffy-colored hair. Why is she looking down on me so angrily? I don't even know her.

Then I begin to make out the other figure standing just behind her. It's a boy, in long skinny-legged jeans. A cigarette, curling smoke, rests between his fingers at his side. Before I even glance at his face, my stomach does a sickening flip-flop. I haven't seen Alex Kirby in two weeks at least. Maybe that's because I haven't been around the court very much. Or maybe I've just been lucky. I'd almost begun to believe he had disappeared, vanished like a bad dream. And suddenly here he is, in the Willises' court, of all places. How come?

The girl is now directing her gaze just past me. Her eyes are on Erica, contentedly playing in the patch of garden.

"That's the little kid I was telling you about," the girl says over her shoulder to Alex. "Erica. She's cute, huh?"

Alex nods and takes a deep drag on his cigarette. All this time he's looking at me with an evil half-grin. He points his cigarette at me and says, "Well, well."

The girl still doesn't realize we know each other. Her glance shifts back to me and she says coldly, "I'm Claudia."

"Hi," I mumble, uncertain as to what's coming next. "My name's Marleen."

"Yeah," she responds. "I know. You're the one who kicked me out of a job."

I blink several times in rapid succession. Her voice is so flat and hard, her accusation so startling. How come she seems to know about me and I don't even know who she is?

"Yeah," she repeats. "I used to be Erica's babysitter. I know her from when she was real little. Her mom really trusted me. Then, all of a sudden, a couple of months ago, you came pushing your way in. Lately, Mrs. Willis hasn't called me once." She scowls, shaking an accusing finger at me. "No, not *once* since you came on the scene. And me," she adds, tapping her chest sharply and waving her other hand in the direction of the apartments, "I live right here in the court, just a couple of doors away."

Awkwardly, I get to my feet. I've been feeling so dumb sitting in the kiddie pool like a docile baby while Claudia whoever-she-is gives me a tongue lashing. All this time, Alex is just standing there, one shoulder higher than the other, his thumb tucked into his trouser belt. He seems to be enjoying my discomfort, and why not? He surely hates me as much as I hate him.

"I . . . I never even heard of you," I protest to Claudia. Actually, it was one of my teachers who'd recommended me to Mrs. Willis. I never thought of myself as having done somebody else out of a job. But if Mrs. Willis had wanted to change baby-sitters, she must have had a reason.

Claudia's hot eyes are on Erica again. I'm sure she doesn't want to hear any explanations from me. And why should I feel I have to give her any?

"And now, just *look*," Claudia exclaims, her lip curling. "The kid's eating dirt. She's got it smeared all over her face. Wow, what a baby-sitter *you* are!" She turns to Alex and jabs him in the stomach with her elbow. "Some baby-sitter, huh? On account of *her*, I lost a good job. Right here in my own court. What a creep."

I scramble out of the pool and kneel down immediately beside Erica. She's only a little smeared. But of course Claudia's looking for something to make a fuss about. I dip the edge of the towel in the pool, wring it out, and clean off the sweet, chubby face. Then I haul Erica up into my arms and hold her to me defensively.

Alex grins at Claudia. "Baby-sitter?" he says with a sputter of laughter. "She ain't no baby-sitter. I know her. She and her old lady moved in my court last winter. I never told you?"

Claudia smiles for the first time. "No, you never told me. You never tell me anything." Her mouth is slightly lopsided and two dents that are not really dimples appear in her cheeks. "You mean to say you know this kid?"

"Yeah," he replies easily. "I know her. And I know somethin' else, too." He pauses to make sure he has Claudia's full attention and, of course, mine as well. "I know how to get her good and mad. Real kickin' and scratchin' mad."

The dents in Claudia's cheeks deepen. Her arms are crossed on her chest and her eyes are brightly fixed on me. "You don't say. A real little spitfire, huh?" She turns her head to Alex's face. "Show me," she says, looking up at him with a flirtatious challenge. "What makes her real mad? Let me see her kick and scratch. That oughtta be fun."

I know—as I've known for a while now—that this is a stand-off and that I'm not going to be able to hold my ground. Besides, there's Erica to think about. I'm holding her so tightly, she's begun to squeal. The key to the Willises' apartment is in my shorts pocket.

With moist fingers I begin probing for it. The pocket is small and shallow. The key should be the first thing I touch. But it doesn't seem to be there. Desperately, I jab deeper, almost tearing my finger through the bottom of the pocket. This time, I feel the key. It's slipped as far as possible to the side.

Abruptly I whirl around and run for the Willises' stoop. I mount the short flight of steps, the heavy baby bouncing and jiggling in my arms.

Claudia finds this hysterically funny. She's broken

out into wild, whooping laughter. Alex, just behind her, is making that braying sound that sends chills down my spine.

I fumble wildly to get the key in the lock. But I'm trembling so badly that I keep swiping at it, far off the mark. Partly this is because Erica is wriggling so hard and keeps screaming in my ear, "Down! I want down!"

All I need to do now is to drop the key altogether. And, blithering idiot that I am, I do.

11

Horror on the Wall

I DON'T KNOW how I've managed to open the door and get Erica and me inside the apartment. Even after I've double-locked it from the inside, I'm still shuddering with helpless rage, and I can hear Alex and Claudia hooting at me in mocking, high-pitched voices, "Ooh, butterfingers! Ooh."

Of course Erica is upset by all this, and she starts crying for her shovel and her rubber duck which we've left outside. My sneakers, Mrs. Willis's towel, and some other things are out there too.

I rush off to the kitchen to get Erica some juice from the refrigerator, hoping that will comfort her. Erica follows me, crying harder now. Probably I'm a terrible failure as a baby-sitter. But what else could I have done to make sure nothing happened to Erica? Claudia might have gone to any lengths to make me look bad, hoping to get her old job back. How do I know? And, as for Alex Kirby . . .

Erica is calmer now as she sips juice from her special cup. I tiptoe back to the living room. It's become strangely quiet outside. Have Alex and Claudia gone? I hope so.

Mrs. Willis keeps the blinds drawn against the afternoon sun, so I can't see out unless I peer between the slats. Carefully, I wriggle into a corner alongside the picture window and gently move one thin metal bar just enough to create a chink for viewing.

The first thing I see is Erica's kiddie pool. There's something floating in it. It's white and sticklike, and I realize with a gasp that it's Alex's doused cigarette. Just the sort of thing he'd do, I think disgustedly.

Then, moving my eye so I can see beyond the pool, I discover that Alex and Claudia are still in the court after all. They're standing a short distance away now, facing each other and speaking so softly that I can't hear them.

They seem to be arguing playfully in whispers. At one point, Claudia shakes her head violently from side to side and beats her fists rapidly against Alex's chest. So Claudia is Alex's girlfriend. Or, if not, they certainly seem to know each other pretty well.

All of a sudden Claudia turns away from Alex with a laughing shriek. He starts chasing her around the empty court. They're playing some sort of tag. I don't know what the stakes are. The whole scene just makes me sick. At the same time, I can't seem to stop watching.

I turn away from the window for a moment to make sure Erica is okay. She's set her juice down on the floor and she's playing with her animal train. I'm relieved to see she's engrossed in her toys and happy again.

All at once, the sound of voices outside comes closer. I turn back hastily to my chink in the blinds.

I'm just in time to see Alex chase Claudia directly into Erica's kiddie pool. Shouting hoarsely, he splashes water on her while she lashes around in the pool on her back trying to kick water in his face.

Of course the water is too shallow to do more than sprinkle Alex. The next moment, Claudia scrambles out of the pool and starts pulling at Alex from behind. He's got hold of the edge of the pool and it's pretty clear he's planning to dump it. Maybe Claudia doesn't want him to. Maybe she's afraid somebody in the court will see her and tell Mrs. Willis.

But suddenly she appears to have changed her mind. She doesn't seem to care. She probably figures she's never going to get back in Mrs. Willis's good graces anyway. So what's the difference? I can hear her counting along with Alex in a very loud, deliberate voice as they pull one side of the kiddie pool up off the ground and get ready for the heave-ho.

"One . . ."

"Two . . ."

"Three!"

The water splashes out the far end onto my sneakers and the other things we've left beside the pool. Everything gets soaked. Then the last of it leaps over into the garden patch of dry soil. The whole thing turns instantly to mud, splattering whatever's in reach with black blobs and blotches.

Triumphantly, Claudia looks up at the Willises' window. Her mouth stretches into a wide smirk. Alex stands beside her, slapping his palms together in satisfied accomplishment.

With a sinking feeling, I realize they've suspected all along that I've been watching them. And, of course, they've dumped the kiddie pool and made a mess for me to clean up out of sheer spite.

I drop to the floor, angry hot tears of frustration stinging my eyes. Impulsively, I reach out for Erica and start hugging her and covering her with kisses. Even as I'm holding the fat, cuddly bundle in my arms, I know that I'm doing it more for my own comfort than for hers.

Three days have gone by, and I'm sitting in Rosalie's bedroom looking at the most astonishing array of horror posters I've ever seen. Her walls are covered with blood and gore, grinning death's heads, black widow spiders, gleaming knives, dripping claws, madmen, freaks, and monsters. It's the first time I've been in the Grants' apartment. Apologetically, Rosalie explains why she's never asked me before.

"We're really just camping out here, so we're not getting into furnishing in a big way." She's lying stomach-down on her bed, heels kicking intermittently in the air. "But I didn't want you to see my room until I got my posters up, the way I used to have them in our old house. Pretty nifty, eh?"

I shift my gaze from a Frankenstein-monster poster to one of the Wolf Man, fangs sprouting from between his lips and clotted blood running down his chin. "I don't see how you can sleep in here nights," I remark.

Rosalie waves her wrist at me. "Oh, I sleep like a baby. The horrors on the wall are as nothing to those that lurk within the human soul. You should know that." She looks at me meaningfully.

I never know if Rosalie is quoting some famous person or if she makes these things up. But they sound good, and she's especially right about the horrors lurking in my human soul these days. I've told Rosalie all about my recent experience with Alex Kirby and Claudia, and she's agreed with me that I've got to do something. But what?

I shake my head, partly in wonderment, partly in despair. "All these characters," I say, sweeping my arms at the terrifying walls, "and not one of them is any use to me in figuring out how to give Alex Kirby what he deserves."

"Ah, if only I'd been there the other day," Rosalie muses. She springs into a sitting position and punches her fist into the air at an invisible target. "I'd have straightened out that Claudia babe *and* the big bully himself. Boy, we'd have had some showdown. A real zinger." She looks at me fiercely.

"What good is all that now?" I ask wearily. "It's over, Rosalie. And I don't see what I could have done differently. I had to protect myself and run. There was the baby to think about."

"I know, I know," Rosalie says. "Well, they won't catch you in such a vulnerable position again. I mean, baby-sitting and all. We'll see to it. I'm glad you told Mrs. Willis what happened, though. There's no reason *not* to tattle on someone like that Claudia."

"A lot of good it does me," I lament to Rosalie. "Even though Mrs. Willis said she 'understood,' I could tell she was shocked. The point is, if I've got enemies like Claudia and Alex around the place, Mrs. Willis isn't going to hire me anymore either. It's too risky. She'll get some nice grandmotherly older lady to baby-sit. So, you see, Claudia was clever. She did me out of a job too."

I turn away. Suddenly I'm close to tears. "And

I'll miss Erica so much. I really do love that little baby."

"Now see here," Rosalie says smartly. "Let's not get maudlin. Let's get thinking. One thing's for certain. You can't go on being the eternal victim. It's not good for you. It's not even good for your enemies. It just makes bigger bullies out of them."

Rosalie is absolutely right, of course. I can't go on cringing on the outside and seething on the inside. It's just tearing me apart.

Trying to choke back my feelings and blinking hard against the mist before my eyes, I get up and go to the window. Rosalie's bedroom faces directly on to the parking lot behind the court. I hadn't realized this. Our apartment is located at a right angle to the Grants' so we don't have this view.

I gaze down numbly. There are only a few cars in the lot this time of the afternoon. It looks hot and still down there, the sun glinting dully on the metal roofs of the automobiles. Instinctively, I look for Ace Kirby's car. It's there, parked at a careless angle and looking more decrepit than ever.

"What do you see?" Rosalie asks lazily from the bed.

I shake my head. "Nothing really. Just that old load that belongs to you-know-who. I wonder if it even runs anymore. To think that my mother had to go and push it that day . . ."

Rosalie bounces off the bed and joins me at the window. "Oh, that," she says, peering down. "It runs all right. But I don't think Ace takes it to work anymore. It just sits around here most days."

I look at Rosalie sharply. "How do you know it runs?"

"Because," Rosalie replies, "I've seen Alex get in it now and then and practice his driving."

I give Rosalie an outraged stare. "Practice his what?"

"Driving, driving," she says matter-of-factly. "What's so strange about that? He usually comes down around nine-thirty in the morning, after the lot's emptied out. Then he starts backing up, doing turns, the usual stuff. After a while, he pulls out into the street. That's when he really goes to town."

"How do you know?" I ask.

"I can hear him," Rosalie says. "He comes to screeching stops. He tries to burn rubber. You know the type. Then, after about five, ten minutes, he comes back. I guess he's scared to do any more. But give him time. He'll get bolder."

I clutch Rosalie's arm. "He's breaking the law, Rosalie. I'm sure he doesn't even have a driving permit."

Rosalie grins. "So what are you going to do about it? Go to the cops? They'll slap him on the wrist and tell him 'no-no.' But he'll go on doing the same thing. Like all the other underage punks. The nights around here are full of the sound of revved-up engines and squealing tires. Or do you sleep with earplugs?"

I turn away from the window and face into Rosalie's bedroom with its walls of horror. If only I could command some of the evil that lurks in the twisted characters on those posters. If only I could aim the striking power of a venomous snake, a deadly scorpion, a spider with a poisonous bite, at Alex Kirby.

"And what's your fertile little mind cooking up now?" Rosalie inquires, sticking her head practically under my chin. "I know. You're thinking of cutting

94

Alex Kirby's brake line. Here's the scenario. He gets into the car, goes shooting out of the parking lot on one of his joy-rides, and finds out too late that he has no brakes. *Crash!* He's hamburger on the dashboard."

I'm still absorbed in my thoughts about the horror posters. I don't even answer Rosalie.

"Oh, sorry," she says, poking her head up even harder under my chin. "That's not quite what you had in mind. You don't want to cut his brake line because he might hurt some innocent person when he smacks up. Good thinking. Considerate. But have you thought about a car bomb? Just a little one. With a timer, so it doesn't go off while he's still in the parking lot. He's just burnt the most delicious streak of rubber, big gooey black marks on the asphalt, that pungent smell delighting his nostrils, when all of a sudden . . . *va-voom. Blast off!* Alex Kirby *and* car are on their way to outer space."

Cutting brakes, planting car bombs. What ideas! Gently, I push Rosalie to one side and advance toward the poster-filled wall opposite the window where we've been standing. I turn to face Rosalie.

"All I want," I say, raising my arms in a regal gesture, "is to be the . . . the queen of all this."

Rosalie tears off her dark glasses and gives me a goggle-eyed look. "The *what?*" she demands.

"The queen," I repeat. "The ruler of hideous forces. So I could do anything I wanted, anything at all. The queen of horror. What do you think?"

"The queen of horror, eh?" Rosalie challenges. "Is that all you want?"

"Um hmmm," I reply dreamily.

Good sport that she is, Rosalie decides to play along with me. "Oh well," she exclaims, "why not?"

With a flourish, she grabs a long ruler off her desk and waves it in the air like the wand of a fairy godmother. Then, very solemnly, she advances toward me and taps me lightly on the right shoulder. "Very well," she declares, "I hereby dub thee 'Marleen, the Horror Queen'!"

12

Selfish Problems

BOBBIE AND I are having a polite argument. At least, that's what it's starting out as.

It's still pretty early in the morning, just after Bobbie's run and her shower. I've already eaten breakfast and started to work on the sweatwear accounts at the other end of the dinette table.

Bobbie has glanced over my shoulder approvingly and headed for the blender, when she suddenly announces that she and I are driving down to the shore tomorrow.

I look up startled. "Tomorrow? Tomorrow's Tuesday."

"I know," Mom says, as the blender starts whirling. "We'll go for Tuesday and Wednesday. Be back Thursday, maybe Friday at the latest."

I'm surprised. We've never gone home in the middle of the week before, and not for longer than two days. Mom's always had to work on the weekdays. Is she softening up, thinking of moving back for good? What's happening?

I shake my head. "I have to work at THE GENTLE PAUSE this week. Mrs. Bigelow's on vacation. Rosalie and her mother are counting on me."

Mom smiles into the brew she's just taken out of the blender. "Oh, I think they can give you a little time off to see your family. You've been working all summer, babe. Don't you think you deserve a break?"

I'm full of confused feelings. Not going to the thrift shop means missing a chance to see Duncan. Any time now he might decide he's had it with the used furniture fixups, and then I might never see him again. I already feel he's been hanging on there because of me, and I'm still trying to work out a way of talking to him when Rosalie isn't around.

Besides, I'm not at all sure I want to go home for a visit. Ever since the last time, I've been nursing a grudge against Neil for the mean way he and Yolanda acted and against Pop, I guess, for not standing up to Mom when I suggested I'd like to stay with him for the summer.

I shake my head again. "There's a sweatwear party on Friday night," I remind Mom.

She sits down blithely and starts her breakfast. "I know," she says. "We'll be back in time for that. Why are you trying to find excuses, Marleen? I thought you'd be thrilled to get away from here for a while, swim in the ocean to your heart's content."

I look up from the accounts. "You go," I say. "It's just not the right time for me. I have . . . things I have to do around here."

Bobbie snaps her dark eyes at me, partly in amusement. "Mysterious, mysterious," she murmurs. "What are you and Rosalie up to these days?"

I ignore her question. "You're just as mysterious," I

reply. "What are you going home for? And in the middle of the week, too?"

Bobbie frowns slightly. "Don't say 'you.' Say 'we.' Because you *are* coming with me, you know."

In a flash, Bobbie's tone of command has made me furious. My words leap at her.

"I told you," I shout, shocked to hear the half-hysterical note in my own voice, "I'm not going. If you want to go to soothe your conscience, then go. I'm not the one who walked out on Pop and Neil. You did! I don't owe them anything."

Bobbie has risen from the table. She looks deeply stricken. A trembling freckled hand clutches at her chest. I stare at her in a kind of terror at what I've said.

Amazingly her voice is very quiet when she speaks. "You resent me that much, don't you, Marleen," she says in a hoarse whisper. "You've never really tried to understand what I'm doing. You've never given me any support at all, have you?"

I feel bewildered, struck dumb, and in some way betrayed. If Bobbie had slapped me hard across the face for the way I've just talked to her, I'd have expected it. But not this awful despair.

She sinks back down at the table. I don't think I've ever seen her shoulders slumped in defeat the way they are now. Almost as though she were talking to herself, she mutters, "I had hoped that . . . well, as a woman, you might have sympathized a little with my need to prove myself. But, of course, you're not a woman. You're just a kid, a teenage kid who's caught up in her own selfish problems. That's how kids are. So why should you be different?" Her voice is almost inaudible now. "I guess I made a mistake," she mumbles. "I expected too much."

I feel paralyzed as I grope for something to say. I want to tell her that whether I understand what she's doing or not, she ought to be able to see that *she's* caught up in selfish problems, too.

And her problems have caused me more trouble than mine have caused her. She's broken up the family, dragged me to a new place to live, a new school, forced me to look for new friends, and been the cause of my nightmarish problems with Alex Kirby. Yet I've tried to keep my growing misery to myself. And I've uncomplainingly helped her with the sweatwear business. But none of that's enough for Bobbie . . .

I glance down at the accounts I've been working on and, in a sudden rush of frustration, I shove the heavy order book away from me. It teeters for a moment at the edge of the table and then goes crashing to the floor.

Bobbie lifts her head sharply. I meet her look and we confront each other silently and urgently. I want desperately for her to see my side of things. Do I really have to spell it all out for her?

As I watch her, something in her eyes tells me that she does know what I've been thinking. Bobbie has that uncanny gift of being able to read my mind.

A moment later she gets up, comes around to my side of the table, and calmly picks up the order book. Maybe it's her athlete's training that makes it possible for her to get hold of herself so quickly after a hot and heavy argument.

"Okay," she says, with an air of having settled things rather than one of resignation. "Okay. I guess you could say that we've both been caught up in selfish problems. You're you and I'm me, so naturally they're different. I'll try to give you some space, baby."

A vast sense of relief sweeps over me. "I don't have to go then?"

"No. Not if you don't want to. But you can't stay in the apartment alone. Either get Rosalie to stay here with you nights or find out if you can stay at her place."

I nod. "That's no problem."

"And I'll try to be back on Thursday. It really all depends on the bank."

"Bank?" I've started to do the accounts again. "What bank?"

"The one in town, back home. That's why I've got to go on a weekday. Your father's promised to co-sign a loan with me." Bobbie bends down and briskly riffles the pages of the order book. "Where do you suppose I'm going to get the money to order in our fall line of sweatwear? This business has taken off like a rocket. Can't let it fizzle out now."

A few moments later, Bobbie dashes out of the room to get dressed. So that's why she's going home. *And* in the middle of the week. It all comes clear to me in a jiffy. She's been on the phone with Pop making business arrangements. As for her softening up, feeling increasingly conscience-stricken about having left Pop and Neil on their own, I was totally wrong in my suspicions. In fact, she and Pop may even be getting on a lot better these days as long-distance business partners with the miles between them.

I get up from the table and peer out the window at the early morning, still-empty court. I guess I'm going to be around here for a while longer, I tell myself. And one thing is certain. I've got my work cut out for me.

* * *

Seven-four-three-dash . . . What am I doing? I'm standing at the wall phone in our kitchen, punching in the first three digits of Duncan's number. If I punch in three more, I'm still safe. But after the seventh one, I'm committed—provided, of course, that the line isn't busy and somebody answers.

Why am I calling Duncan? I've never called a boy before in my life. At least, not since third grade. I think there's a kind of panic in me. I knew something like this was going to happen. Yesterday, after my argument with Mom, Rosalie and I and Rosalie's mother went to THE GENTLE PAUSE to work as usual. For the first time in weeks, Duncan didn't show up at all.

I tried not to say anything about it. But, of course, Rosalie commented.

"Looks like your secret lover's deserted you," she grinned. "Or hadn't you noticed?"

"Oh," I said airily, trying to think of a logical excuse for Duncan's absence, "maybe he's gone on vacation with his aunt."

Rosalie gave me a look of pity and shook her head. "Not likely," she remarked. "Mr. and Mrs. Bigelow happen to have gone on a trip to the Orient. I doubt if they were planning to take their fifteen-year-old nephew, Duncan Donuts, along with them."

I shrugged. "Well, maybe he feels sort of shy coming around when his aunt's away."

"Ha!" Rosalie snorted. "Baloney."

I decided not to say another word. There was something just a tiny bit unpleasant in Rosalie's tone. Was she gloating because Duncan and she had never gotten along very well and she was glad he'd disappeared at last?

The hours went by. For some reason the shop was

102

busy. We sold lots of paperback books and all the bamboo, plastic, and paper fans in the place. We even sold an old canvas hammock that smelled of mildew and that Rosalie's mother said had been sitting around for years. It seemed pretty clear that everyone expected August to be just as hot as July. Maybe hotter.

Around four o'clock, things finally got quiet. Rosalie was in the back room digging some more paperbacks out of the cartons where we stored them. I was in the front part of the shop, straightening the picked-over book bins.

Suddenly my glance lighted on Mrs. Bigelow's desk, the tiny one with the chipped carvings where she usually sat untangling and tagging jewelry. An idea had been fluttering at the back of my mind all afternoon. In the top drawer, Mrs. Bigelow kept a neat, small pile of Duncan's "business" leaflets, the ones that said:

SQUIRRELS AND OTHER PROPERTY PESTS
Humanely caught and far-released
Phone for prices

My heart pounding, I stole a glance backward to the room where Rosalie was working. Then, as stealthily as a midnight thief, I carefully opened the creaking little drawer, snatched up one of the leaflets, folded it into a lopsided square, and wedged it deep, deep down into the pocket of my jeans. By the time I fell asleep last night, I had Duncan's "Phone for prices" telephone number memorized as perfectly as if it had been engraved on my forehead.

This morning, after Bobbie left for the shore at the crack of dawn, I began to "psych" myself up for the phone call to Duncan. Why shouldn't I phone him, I asked myself? It's just the natural, simple, polite thing to do. Maybe he's sick, maybe he's had an accident. He could have been bitten by a squirrel, a raccoon, even a field mouse. His work as a humane catcher of property pests is not, after all, undangerous.

I rehearsed a few opening lines. They all sounded stilted and forced. I went through the possibilities of who might answer the phone. If Duncan had a mother, a father, and one brother or sister, there was probably a less than twenty-five percent chance that he would be the one to answer. Suppose he wasn't home at all. What sort of message should I leave, if any?

By a quarter to nine, I couldn't stand it any longer. All those smiles from Duncan whenever I came into view, those wide-eyed looks of interest and pleasure— they *had* to mean something. I couldn't just let Duncan walk out of my life without letting him know, in an indirect way, of course, that I'd noticed, that I cared, that I did want to continue our friendship.

Seven-four-three-dash . . . And now the next four numbers . . .

It's ringing, it's ringing! Mom told me yesterday that I was just a teenage kid caught up in her own selfish problems. I don't think I'm being selfish in calling Duncan, in trying to find out how he is. But maybe I am. Because I do want to talk to him.

Only I'm so scared. And now the ringing's stopped and there's that most terrible moment of all, that instant of silence right after somebody picks up the phone at the other end and just before they say hello.

13

The Cave

"HELLO?"

The voice is unmistakable. It isn't Duncan's mother or sister. It's doubtful his father would sound like that. Unless he has a twin brother, it's Duncan himself. The pang of recognition sends tremors through my body. "Is this Duncan?"

"Yes." He sounds tentative, not sure of who he's talking to.

I have to take the plunge. "This is Marleen. Um, from the thrift shop."

"Marleen."

There's a horrible instant of suspense. Suppose he doesn't remember who I am. Suppose my name doesn't mean anything at all to him. Maybe I ought to hang up right now, act like it's been a great big mistake. . . .

Then his voice is crackling warmly all around me. "Marleen. Hi." I can *hear* him smiling, his teeth gleaming like Chiclets. Duncan doesn't look like anybody's idea of a romance hero, far from it. But he's so open and straightforward. I like that. Duncan doesn't play games.

"We, ah, all missed you at the shop yesterday," I say, trying to keep things impersonal. "Is everything okay with you?"

"Sure, sure," he responds heartily. "Gee, I'm glad you called, Marleen."

There's an awkward pause. What should I say now? Maybe conversation's never going to be easy with Duncan, even without Rosalie around.

"I guess you've been working, catching squirrels and . . . things," I suggest.

"That's right," Duncan replies. "I had a job yesterday. Got five. Then the lady asked me to come back today."

I'm silent. That means he won't be coming to the shop today either. All I can manage to utter is "Oh."

"Funny thing," Duncan says. "You live over in the garden apartments, don't you?"

I wonder how Duncan knew that. Maybe he found out from his aunt, who learned it from Rosalie's mother. "Yes," I say.

"Well, this property where I've been working, it's right near the apartments. A very big old house, the Weller place. Lots of ground. Maybe you know it. The owners had a chance to sell to the developer, but they wouldn't. Now they're sorry."

"Oh," I say, thinking maybe I do know the house. Its yard backs on one of the parking lots. "Why are they sorry?"

"Well," Duncan replies in a professional-sounding drawl, "they've got a rodent problem. Inside as well as out. Know what I mean?"

I shudder slightly. "They've got mice in the house?"

Duncan clears his throat. "A little worse."

"Rats!" I declare in a breathless gasp.

"You got it," Duncan says calmly.

What a conversation, I think to myself. But at least we're talking.

"Listen," Duncan says with a sudden burst of enthusiasm, "I've got to go over there in a little while. Set up my squirrel trap. Maybe you'd want to walk over. I could show you, er, how it's done. It's a pretty nice garden. Big shade trees."

Instantly I break into a sweat and try to think very fast. The part about catching a few squirrels that are going to be transported doesn't bother me. It's not too horrible. But I'm supposed to go to THE GENTLE PAUSE with Rosalie around noon when it opens. Still, there's lots of time. If only I can sneak out of the court without running into her.

"Well," I answer, trying not to sound too eager. "I guess I could do that."

"Great!" Duncan exclaims. I can tell he's really happy about it. "Now are you sure you know the place I mean? Let me give you the address."

It's arranged that Duncan's going to bike over there with his trap and we're to meet in twenty minutes.

I spend the next quarter of an hour changing tops to wear with my jeans and rearranging my hair. It's gotten a little sunbleached and thicker-looking this summer. The high humidity has even begun to curl the short ends I cut around my forehead. Here and there, there's the faintest suggestion of a tendril.

When I get downstairs, I take a last quick look into the court. I've already decided which exit I'll use to get out to the street as quickly as possible. To my surprise, Mrs. Hofmeier is sitting on her stoop, looking as though she's been sprawled there forever. Yet, when I peered out of our front window a few moments earlier, she was nowhere in sight. Now there's no avoiding her.

Mrs. Hofmeier is still wearing her bedroom slippers, and her nightgown is peeking out from under a short, flowered housecoat. I've never seen her dressed this way. Her bare legs are veined with purple and mottled almost black around the ankles.

She gazes up at me almost imploringly. "I just *had* to get out of the apartment," she explains, without her usual greeting. "There's not a breath of air in there, not a breath. I thought it'd be better out here. But I don't know. I just don't know."

Her face is pasty. Even holding up her head to talk to me seems an effort. And there are no questions like "Where are you off to in this heat, dear?" No remarks like "Your mother certainly drove off at an early hour this morning, didn't she?" Nothing at all.

For a moment, I feel like confiding in Mrs. Hofmeier, asking her to please not tell Rosalie that she saw me leave the court. But she appears to have wandered off into thoughts of her own. The court gossip, the sharp-eyed terror of the beach-chair brigade, seems strangely harmless this morning.

"I think I just felt a breeze spring up, Mrs. Hofmeier," I say, trying to offer encouragement. "Maybe the heat will break today." And with that I'm off, running on winged feet to meet Duncan.

"The smell," Mrs. Weller is saying. "The awful sickening smell. It's the smell of death and decomposition. Do you know what I'm saying?"

Duncan and I are standing in the cavernlike cellar of

the old house beside the garden apartment development. We arrived at the Weller place a short while ago and Duncan set up his baited squirrel trap in the garden. Then, before either of us could catch our breath, Mrs. Weller, the owner, came out and asked Duncan if he would mind giving her his opinion about something. Duncan introduced me and we all three went inside the house.

Mrs. Weller is a tall, thin woman with short, stylishly cut gray hair. We're all sniffing like mad, trying to decide where the terrible, slightly sweet odor of decay is coming from. The basement is spooky all right. It's full of little alcoves. The lights Mrs. Weller has turned on throw long, twisted shadows. Most of them end abruptly in one of the dark caves that lie at opposite ends of the cellar. Mrs. Weller has explained that these "caves" are earthen dugouts under a pair of porches.

What a setting for a horror movie, I think to myself. Anything could be lurking in those caves. Imagine being forced to spend a night down here all by yourself. I wish Rosalie could see this place. But, of course, I can't even tell her about it. I'd never want her to know about my phoning Duncan and getting together with him at one of his "jobs."

As soon as I saw Duncan this morning, all of my worries vanished. I knew right away that as long as it was just the two of us, we were going to get along fine. His smile was full of reassurance, so I was right in trying to see him without Rosalie being around.

The odor is definitely stronger near one of the caves, so Mrs. Weller goes upstairs to get fresh batteries for the flashlight she's brought down. So far, its pale yellow beam has been too faint to show us very much inside the cave.

"What do you think it is?" I whisper to Duncan while Mrs. Weller is gone.

Duncan tosses back his head. "Sewer rats, maybe. They could tunnel their way into that cave from the outside pipes. Easy to burrow through the damp earth."

I can barely suppress a screech. "Would they come into this part of the cellar too, then?"

"Sure," Duncan replies matter-of-factly. "Why not?"

There's a chest-high opening into the cave, big enough for a person to wriggle through, so I guess he's right. I jump away from the spot where I've been standing. Did I just feel the flick of a long, hairless tail on my calf, the nick of a sharp fang at my ankle?

Duncan grabs my upper arm. "Take it easy, Marleen. Are you okay?"

I nod through clenched teeth.

His arm encircles my shoulder comfortingly. His eyes gaze earnestly at my face. "I'm sorry. I didn't mean to get you into this. I had no idea she'd ask me to come down here on this kind of job. But there's nothing to worry about. Whatever's been scurrying around in that cave is dead for sure."

"*And* rotting," I add. Even as I speak the smell seems to be getting stronger. "What do you think killed those rats?"

"Rat poison probably," Duncan answers softly, removing his arm from my shoulder. Overhead we can hear Mrs. Weller's steps. She'll probably be coming back down any minute now.

"Most people don't like to admit it when they use the stuff," Duncan adds in a hasty whisper. "I've seen

110

this happen before. The poisoning part is easy, though. It's getting rid of the dead bodies that's creepy. Especially if they die in some place where you can't get at 'em easily."

Mrs. Weller returns, apologizing for how long it took her to find the new batteries. "I never know where Mr. Weller squirrels things away," she says with a sigh of exasperation. "He's such a *rat-packer.*" Then, taken aback at her own choice of words, she winces and cups her hand across her mouth.

By this time, I'm feeling so paralyzed with foreboding that I stay where I am while Mrs. Weller and Duncan go forward to examine the cave. The beam is bright and penetrating now. Silently they peer in, heads together, through the chest-high opening.

All of a sudden Mrs. Weller utters a high-pitched shriek. She turns and comes skittering toward me on long, thin legs, her entire body twitching. As she grabs me, I too begin to shriek. I'm engulfed in the terror that has attacked Mrs. Weller. We cling to each other, caterwauling like a couple of banshees.

"I saw them, I saw them!" Mrs. Weller howls in a raw, quivering voice. "A whole family, I think. Maybe seven or eight. It's like a mass murder scene. Oh, I told Mr. Weller to call in a professional exterminator. But no, he said he'd take care of it himself. Now he's off on a business trip and I'm left with *this!*"

In her agitation, Mrs. Weller clutches at me even more tightly. Then, suddenly shamed, she releases me and backs away wringing her hands. "I'm so sorry," she gasps, "to be carrying on this way." Her face is white, her eyes wild. "I'm usually a very controlled person. But this is too much. I'm so . . . perturbed."

"It's . . . okay," I tell her. Compared to Mrs. Weller, I'm almost calm. But I'm awfully embarrassed. All that screaming I did with her. What must Duncan be thinking? That all women are ninnies, I suppose.

Sympathetically, Duncan walks Mrs. Weller to the basement stairs and agrees to take the job of clearing out the cave right away. She gets him a shovel and some heavy plastic bags and departs gratefully.

Duncan returns to where I've been standing. His eyes question me. Do I want to leave too?

Ripples of horror are still running through me. I don't know what to answer. I didn't see what Mrs. Weller saw inside the cave. But even if I had, I tell myself, is seeing a few dead rats really so terrible?

It's horrible, yes. This shadowy basement with all its dark recesses is horrible. But if I've prayed to be a queen of horror, somebody who can control the forces of evil and use them for her own purposes, I'm going to have to stop quaking and shivering over something like this. I must try to prove I'm worthy of being—as Rosalie put it—"Marleen, the Horror Queen."

"If I . . . stayed," I say hesitantly, "could I help?"

Duncan releases a sharp breath of air and I suddenly realize that he's scared too. He locks his fingers around my wrist, and I know it's a sign of his gratitude and relief.

"Thanks," he says in a husky whisper.

The fact that he needs me here makes me feel stronger. Neither of us utters another word. Together we approach the cave.

Duncan hands me the flashlight and the plastic bags Mrs. Weller's given him for the dead rats. He picks up the shovel and tosses it into the cave. Then he scrambles up the wall, wriggles his chest and shoulders through the opening, and sinks bellydown onto the damp, foul-smelling earth.

As I get ready to shine the flashlight ahead of him on to the scattered corpses he's about to collect, I pray for courage—the courage of a horror queen.

14

A Late-Night Walk

ALTHOUGH I TRIED to tell Mrs. Hofmeier that the weather might break today, it hasn't. Tonight is as ominously still as this morning was. There's an eerie sense of waiting that just hangs in the air along with the stifling heat.

It's now eleven P.M. and Rosalie and I have just finished watching a horror movie on TV. I was invited to dinner at the Grants' apartment this evening because of Mom's being away, and I'm supposed to sleep at Rosalie's tonight.

Rosalie snaps off the late evening news and says, "Let's go out for a breath of—ha-ha—air. We can talk. Maybe discuss the stupendous film we just viewed."

I glance at Rosalie warily. If she noticed anything odd or different about me during our afternoon of working together at THE GENTLE PAUSE, she didn't mention it. Perhaps she was too zonked by the heat to notice much. She didn't even say anything about Duncan not showing up for the second day in a row.

Even though it's late, the court is still dotted with

little clusters of people sitting on folding chairs in front of the apartment stoops. Mrs. Hofmeier, though, must have given up earlier and gone to bed. The place where she usually sits with her regular group of attendants is vacant.

"What a crummy movie," Rosalie remarks grouchily as we head out of the court and into the street.

"All that blood," I comment. "They must have used tons of ketchup." The story had taken place at a summer camp. A ten-year-old camper who was supposed to have drowned in the lake years ago comes back as a grown-up axe murderer. He knocks off the counselors one by one, each in a different horrible way.

"Blood doesn't mean a thing," Rosalie sniffs. "It's horror that counts. Real honest-to-goodness horror. And that movie was a first-class dud. They sure don't make 'em like they used to."

Since I'm just a newcomer to the horror-movie scene, I don't even know what to look for. I haven't seen all the old-time horror classics that Rosalie has and that she keeps hinting are so great. I wonder if she would have considered this morning horrible. All day I've been reliving our experience, Duncan's and mine, in Mrs. Weller's basement. The sticky-sweet odor of decay still lingers sickeningly in my nostrils. I'd almost have expected that Rosalie would catch the scent.

We're walking on a street now that fringes the last of the garden apartments. Across the way are large stone houses set back on darkened lawns heavily shadowed by trees. The houses are dimly lit within. The only sound that comes from them is the insistent whir of their air-conditioners, humming with a steady rhythm like that of the cicadas all this summer.

"Let's cross," Rosalie suggests. "Somehow it looks cooler over on that side. More open spaces."

These houses remind me of the Weller place, which isn't far from here either. They, too, probably have dark, old-fashioned cellars, cellars infested with spiders, strange crawling bugs, and maybe even large, furry . . . rodents. I shiver in spite of the heat as I think of the scene in the Weller basement—me beaming the flashlight on to the partly rotted corpses, Duncan shoveling the limp but surprisingly heavy remains into the shiny black plastic bags and handing them to me one by one through the hole in the cave, the two of us working together all the while in well understood silence.

We follow Rosalie's suggestion, and she and I cross the empty street. Just as we are about to step onto the curb, the late-night quiet is shattered by a car that swerves screechily around the corner and bears down in our direction. Instinctively we turn to look and are almost blinded by the glare of the headlights. As the car passes swiftly with a strong whoosh of air, I'm sure I hear a faint shout from within.

"Who was *that?*" I demand, suddenly wide-eyed with suspicion and alarm.

Rosalie hunches her shoulders. "Beats me. I couldn't see a thing."

"I know," I say. "I couldn't see either. But I thought I heard something. As though somebody called out."

"Maybe a radio playing," Rosalie offers.

"I don't think so," I reply. "I heard a voice. I'm pretty sure I *know* who it was."

"Oh Marleen," Rosalie says with faint annoyance. "There you go again. You know what this reminds me of? That first time I walked you over to THE GENTLE PAUSE. A car came squealing around the corner and you kept insisting it was Alex Kirby and his brother, trying to kill you. And it wasn't even their car. Or them."

"Rosalie!" I reply huffily, "I never said they were trying to kill me. That was your idea. I just said it was their car. And you never proved it wasn't."

"And you," Rosalie says, shaking a finger at me, "never proved it was."

Rosalie and I are standing on the curb now beside a long gravel-topped driveway. The curbside is laden with several large plastic trash bags waiting for the next sanitation pickup. I can't look at them without thinking of Duncan and me dragging the bags from Mrs. Weller's cellar to the edge of her property for the same reason—to wait for the next garbage collection. Where, after all, was Duncan going to take them?

"Oh, why are we standing here arguing?" Rosalie remarks with an impatient shrug. "All I'm trying to tell you, Marleen, is that this town—the whole world for that matter—is full of punk kids driving around on two wheels trying to show off the muscles in their heads. So you can't assume that every one of them is Alex Kirby. You know, I've been thinking a lot about that 'horror queen' stuff you were talking about the other day. And, if you want my opinion, revenge is for . . . for the movies. In real life, it would be nothing but a hollow victory. At best."

I give Rosalie a stony look. How could I ever have been so foolish as to share my fantasies with her? Rosalie doesn't really understand about revenge because actually she's a whole lot like Bobbie. I honestly think Rosalie *likes* being a little freaky and attracting attention, no matter what kind. I've long suspected that's how Mom feels. No matter what she says, she really glories in rippling those muscles of hers and hearing the roar of the crowd. It doesn't seem fair, though, that someone like me who's always trying to blend into the scenery should get picked on so much. Or that I should be blamed for having that burning need to get even.

Mom's always said I'm too self-conscious and it's mainly my imagination. Is that what Rosalie's trying to tell me too?

"Okay," I say, trying not to sound hurt, just indifferent. "Forget everything I said, all that 'horror queen' talk. I was just kidding anyway."

"No you weren't," Rosalie insists stubbornly. "I know you, Marleen. I just don't want to see you take things too far. You'd only get hurt even more in the end."

"So?" I say defiantly, "why should *you* care?"

We're still standing in the same place, beside the garbage bags at the curb. We're not ready to continue our walk, it seems, until we get ourselves sorted out.

"You know what?" Rosalie announces, smiling faintly but looking at me grimly through her dark lenses, "I think we're having our first big fight. Now, how are we going to spend the whole night together in my chamber of horrors?"

"We aren't," I snap at her. I whip the keys to our apartment out of my jeans pocket and jingle them in front of Rosalie's forehead which is just about level with my chin. "There's no reason I can't sleep at home alone tonight," I declare. "If Dracula comes for me, I'll just stick my head out the window and scream.

That should bring about fifty nosybody neighbors running."

"Don't count on it," Rosalie says drily. "People have a way of ignoring things when they want to. Anyhow, you promised your mother you wouldn't stay alone. Even if we're not talking to each other, I could come over to your place and sleep in the living room."

I've begun shaking my head in a firm gesture of "never mind" when a pair of headlights comes beaming at us from around the same corner as before. Again, the too-bright lights sweep down the street in our direction. But this time the car is moving silently, cruising slowly. The first car went by much too fast. This one is altogether too slow.

Transfixed, Rosalie and I squint into the glare, our fingers suddenly entwined. I can feel Rosalie's sharply curved nails digging into the palm of my hand.

Why are we just standing here? Why don't we run up to the door of one of the houses with the dim lights and the humming air-conditioners? Maybe Rosalie is right about the car that went by before. Maybe it didn't have anything at all to do with Alex Kirby. If this is the same car, we may be in even more danger than we know. It's entirely too lonely here on this street in the muffled darkness.

As the car creeps closer, I see that the window on the passenger's side is rolled down. But it's too dim to make out anything at all within. Even the dashboard lights must be off. The driver is in deep shadow.

I can hear Rosalie breathing hard beside me. It occurs to me that even if we rang the doorbell of one of the houses there's a good chance that nobody would answer at this late hour. Or there might not even be anybody at home. People leave lights on to keep burglars away. They leave air-conditioners on to keep their pets cool. We mustn't get trapped in some spot that's even more deserted, even more dangerous than this one.

That's what kept happening to the victims of the axe murderer in the horror movie we saw on TV tonight. They actually set themselves up for their own deaths. How could they have been so dumb?

I tug sharply at Rosalie's arm, silently urging her to think of something. But I get no response from her. And then, all at once, the car is abreast of us.

"Hey," a voice says from the darkness deep inside. "I'm looking for a baby-sitter. Hey you, the tall skinny one. Are you a baby-sitter?"

Relief and anger sweep over me at the exact same moment. The driver of the car is not an axe murderer, not some terrifying new neighborhood strangler who's just getting his act together and has picked Rosalie and me as his first victims.

No, it's my old familiar enemy. Even though Alex Kirby is trying to disguise his voice, to make it sound deeper, older, and slightly sinister, I can tell at once it's he.

And I can tell, too, now that the car is directly alongside us, that it's the same old rotting maroon load that has belonged to Alex's brother all along. The only thing that's different now is that, even though I'm sure he hasn't got a license, Alex himself is driving.

Brazenly, I step off the curb, dragging Rosalie along with me.

"Very funny," I say, going directly up to the open window of the car. "Only maybe you heard. I'm not a baby-sitter anymore. You and your girlfriend took care of that."

"What a cruddy thing that was to do," Rosalie chimes in, suddenly finding her voice and deciding, I guess, to let Alex have it. "Teasing somebody who was taking care of a helpless little baby, dumping the baby's kiddie pool all over everything. Why don't you GROW UP!"

"And why don't you *shut* up?" Alex spits back at her. He's dropped his act of sinister-driver-in-the-slowly-moving-car and sounds exactly like his old ugly, braying self.

"You oaf!" Rosalie shouts at him. "Pea-brain. Imbecile. Retard. Creep." She's going all-out this time. Maybe she feels she owes it to me because of the argument she and I have been having.

But I just know that calling Alex Kirby names isn't good enough. Whether Rosalie agrees with me or not, there has to be . . . revenge.

"Ahh, can't you shut that squirt up?" Alex asks, addressing me directly. He's trying for that suave act again, sitting back at the wheel like a big-time gangster. "I just wanted to say," he goes on in a strangely droning voice, "that I'm real sorry you ain't a baby-sitter anymore. And, uh, also that I'm sorry that, uh, the kiddie pool got dumped over onto the dirt."

What *is* this, I ask myself, in shock and amazement. Is Alex Kirby making some kind of a rehearsed speech of apology to me? I can't believe it. Even Rosalie has become quiet. Her mouth is actually hanging open. We both draw a little closer to the open window of the car, trying to peer across to the driver's side so we can see Alex's expression. Can this really be happening?

"And," he drawls on, "to, uh, make up for gettin' your clothes and stuff dirty . . ."

Something is wrong here. Rosalie has spotted it first. She ducks down sharply beneath the window opening and attempts to pull me with her. But her quick try doesn't work. My chin gets bumped against the lower edge of the car window and I'm stuck there. Before I can pull back, I see that a hunched figure—a figure that's been coiled into a crouch on the floor in front of the passenger seat—has sprung up onto the seat. There is hysterical, shrieking laughter. And the next moment I'm shot full in the face with a stream of water from a high-powered water gun.

My eyes feel like they've been plugged against the back of my skull, my nose feels mashed, and my tongue wobbles helplessly in a sea of gurgles. Rosalie is screaming new and more horrible names at Alex, while at the same time trying to pull me away from the car with both arms.

Suddenly the engine explodes in a roar and the car takes off at high speed, its tires emitting an ear-piercing squeal. I rub savagely at my water-shot eyes and, by the faint light of a street lamp near the corner, I catch a quick glimpse of the person who squirted the gun at me.

Of course, I tell myself. I should have known!

It was Claudia. Her head is hanging out the window now and she's looking back at me, her taffy hair flying and mean laughter pouring from her lips.

15

An Early-Morning Mission

IT'S A QUARTER past five the next morning. Rosalie is sleeping in Bobbie's room. She insisted on staying here with me last night because she said I was hysterical.

"I'm not," I told her. "Do you see me shrieking and howling? Do you see me tearing my hair out?"

"That's the whole trouble," Rosalie replied as we mounted the staircase to the apartment after picking up Rosalie's pajamas at her place and notifying her mother of our change in plans. "You're too quiet. It's not natural. I think you're still in shock."

"I'm shocked all right," I told her. "Imagine getting it full in the face at such close range. Oh, why didn't I realize something was up? Why didn't I duck in time? They're not getting away with this, Rosalie. I don't care what you say."

"Okay, okay," Rosalie murmured soothingly as I unlocked the door of the apartment. "We'll think of something. Whew, it's hot in here. Where's the nearest air-conditioner?"

We must have talked for nearly an hour in Bobbie's room before we went to sleep. Once or twice, Rosalie nodded off, sitting opposite me, cross-legged on the bed. Of course, it was a little hard to tell for sure what was going on behind those dark glasses. Sometimes I wondered if she slept in them.

We agreed that the first car, the one that had gone speeding through the street, had also been Alex's.

"He and Claudia might have seen us leaving the court," Rosalie suggested, "and decided to follow us. Or maybe he just came down that street by chance and recognized us. After I saw him go out practicing in the mornings, I knew it wouldn't be long before he joined the ranks of the neighborhood night riders."

"I wish," I sighed, "I knew why people always pick on me. You can't say it was my imagination, can you?"

"No," Rosalie yawned. "That was one terrific water-gun shot, right smack in the kisser. But remember, they meant it for both of us, not just you. You know, they could have been cruising around all evening, looking for some fun. After all, they're a pair of perfectly matched cretins, Marleen. What can you expect?"

"I don't know," I replied. "But this time I'm going to *do* something. Something really . . . really . . ."

Rosalie's chin was dipping onto her chest again, her glasses slipping down her nose.

I rose gently from the foot of the bed and switched off the lamp. "You can take your glasses off now, Rosalie," I said softly. "Nobody can see a thing."

"Hah!" Rosalie spoke with a start in the darkened room. The next moment I heard the faintest of snores. I closed the door and tiptoed to my own room.

It didn't matter that Rosalie had fallen asleep on me. I didn't need to exchange another word with her about getting even with Alex Kirby. Suddenly I knew exactly what I was going to do. Maybe it wasn't a horror-queen revenge inspired by one of the great horror movies. But it *was* horrible. Horrible enough!

I slept only a few hours, if sleeping was the right word for it. In my state of jumpy semi-drowsiness, I went over every step of my plan. It was simple, astonishingly simple. Of course, I had no supernatural powers, no evil magic, no witchlike spells that I could work against Alex and Claudia. I was just an ordinary mortal, tormented enough to make my final move. And the ingredients were right at hand. Or were they? That was what I had to make absolutely sure of.

So now, at five-fifteen on yet another hot, muggy morning, I find myself softly shutting the door of the apartment and creeping down the stairs to the court.

The air is like a massive cloud of steam. In the grayish-white fog, I flit out of the court and into the parking lot. I've got to work fast. People are up early these days. Some pull out of the parking lot well before six.

Please, I whisper silently to myself, let it be there. After all, they *must* have come back sometime last night.

My eyes sweep across the rows of cars. Maroon . . . maroon, with rusted-out patches on the doors, dents and creases all over the body, a slanted rear bumper that looks like a crooked mouth. Everything about that car reminds me of Alex Kirby. It's everything that he is—and it's perfect for my plan.

The car is there! It's parked crazily as usual, taking up nearly two spaces. I approach it rapidly, yet gin-

125

gerly. I have to know only one thing and I don't want anyone to see me finding it out. I dart across to the door on the passenger side because I'll be more hidden from view there. I take a deep breath and try the door handle.

It turns down easily and I feel sure I can pull it toward me. But suddenly it catches. I'm surprised that it should be locked. When I tried the door on the driver's side of the Kirby car, the night that Mom and I returned from the first sweat party, it was unlocked. Was that just an accident? Is Alex getting more protective of the car now that he's driving it around?

There's only one thing to do. I'll have to walk around the car and try the door on the other side. But first I give one last hard wrench to the passenger-door handle. It creaks and flies open so abruptly that I totter backward and almost lose my balance. I smile with satisfaction and peer inside the car briefly. On the scuffed, torn carpet beneath the passenger seat, the water gun that Claudia used on me last night is lying in a little pool of leaking water.

Perfect! I have just one more thing to do. Closing the car door as quietly as I can, I dash out of the lot and into the street, heading directly for the Weller property. I must be sure to get there before the early-morning garbage pickup and I haven't got a minute to lose.

"Where've you been?" Rosalie demands. She's standing at the top of the stairs in wrinkled pajamas, rubbing her eyes.

I've been gone only about twenty-five minutes. It's probably not even six o'clock yet. I hadn't counted on

Rosalie's waking up before I returned. I didn't plan on having to explain my absence to her.

"You look very strange," Rosalie pounces. "Wait until I go get my glasses."

"Rosalie," I groan, as she stumbles down the hall toward the bedroom, "why don't you just go back to bed? I couldn't sleep so I went out for a little walk. That's all."

Rosalie is back, surveying me from behind those one-way dark lenses of hers. "More like a little *run,* I'd say," she comments. "You're all sweated up, Marleen. And there's a maniacal gleam in your eye. You've been up to some kind of dirty work, I'll bet. Did you plant that time bomb in Alex Kirby's car after all?"

I shake my head violently. "What are you talking about?"

This is too close to the truth for comfort. Is Rosalie psychic, I wonder? Or just very smart? It's frightening being around her sometimes. But, of course, there's no way, I tell myself, that she could possibly know what I've really been up to.

She knows nothing about my meeting Duncan yesterday morning over at the Weller place. She knows nothing about the black plastic garbage bags parked at the edge of the Weller property that I've just rescued from the early-morning sanitation pickup.

Now that I'm back in the apartment, now that my horrible mission is behind me, a terrifying weakness is beginning to creep over me. I drop onto the sofa in the living room. My skin feels clammy. There's a cold sweat on my forehead. And that terrible smell is back in my nostrils, the menacing, sweet, stomach-wrenching smell of decay.

Rosalie parks herself opposite me. We're sitting in exactly the same places where we sat the first time we met, when Rosalie was trying to find out if I was weird enough to be her friend. Well, I think to myself, probably now I'm weird enough. Maybe too weird.

I can hardly believe what I've done. I've gone to the Weller place and dragged back two of the bags that Duncan filled yesterday morning. I chose two of the heaviest, each with several bodies in it.

Getting the bags back to the parking lot and dumping them in the front seat of Alex Kirby's car was *not* the most horrible part of my mission. In spite of the hot weather, the firmly tied bags gave off hardly any of the odor of their foul-smelling contents. But I wasn't going to simply leave the bags in the car unopened. I wasn't going to let Alex off that easily. When he arrived at his car later in the morning, or whenever, I wanted him to experience the full flavor of my message. I wanted him to know exactly what I thought of him.

"You look awful, Marleen," Rosalie says. She hasn't taken her eyes off me since we sat down. "Are you going to be sick? You're turning green. Do you know that?"

I wonder how Rosalie can tell one color from another behind those smoky black lenses. But maybe she's learned. After all, she's had years of practice.

"I'm okay," I say, choking a little as I feel my jaw tightening and my throat beginning to both rise up and close at the same time.

Rosalie leaps off the chair and kneels at my feet. She grabs both my hands.

"What did you *do?*" she screeches. "You did something horrible, Marleen. You'd better tell me. I'm your friend, you dope. Don't you know that? Marleen!"

I can feel Rosalie's meaty little palms slapping at my cheeks. My eyes are wide open but something strange is happening. The room is full of black polka dots. The dots are getting larger. They're becoming so large, in fact, that they're beginning to fuse into huge inky patches. The patches, too, are growing. Soon there will be total blackness.

Just before the last little ragged patch of light disappears, I see again the horror scene as I savagely tore open the plastic bags in Alex Kirby's car and scattered the stinking, rotted corpses of Mrs. Weller's rats across the front seat and the floor. One limp, mangy-furred body fell with perfect justice beside Claudia's water gun, its naked scabby tail flung gracefully across the handle.

The next moment Rosalie's frantic patting at my face seems to fade away and the darkness closes in completely.

16

At Mrs. Hofmeier's

IT'S EARLY AFTERNOON. All morning Rosalie's been treating me like an invalid. After my blackout, which probably didn't last more than a minute or so, she insisted on putting fresh, cool, wet cloths on my forehead every twenty minutes, on taking my temperature three different times, and on making me rest in bed.

I was wobbly at first after I came to, and waves of nausea kept riding over me. I couldn't eat or drink anything. So Rosalie fed me ice chips, placing them gently on my tongue, one by one. She declared that because of the heat I'd dehydrate in a couple of hours if I didn't have any liquids at all.

Later in the morning, I slept a little and felt much better. But even then she wanted to get her mother to come over, to call a doctor, even to phone Bobbie.

"No!" I shouted at her. "Now stop it, Rosalie. I never knew you could be such a pest."

Rosalie grinned. "Ah," she said, "I see you *are* feeling better. Now what should I do about going to the thrift shop this afternoon? With Mrs. Bigelow still away, I know we're going to be shorthanded."

"Go," I urged her. "I'll stay right here and rest some more. I promise."

"You won't, Marleen," she retorted. "I know you. You're up to something. And when I get back, you're going to tell me what it is. Even if I have to use my famous, exquisite, Chinese water-torture method on you. People don't simply come back from a walk at five-thirty in the morning, turn green, and faint. There's too much circumstantial evidence. If you know what I mean."

What a relief it is to watch Rosalie's departing back as she skips down the stairs. It isn't that I'm not grateful to her. I never dreamed I'd pass out after depositing my horrible message in Alex Kirby's car. All the while I was carrying out my mission of revenge, I felt so steady and sure of myself.

Now, of course, with Rosalie out of the way and off to THE GENTLE PAUSE in her mother's car, I'm trembling with anxiety. How will I know what's happened, *if* anything has happened yet? Did Alex get into his car for a practice session this morning after the parking lot emptied, or doesn't he do that anymore? Now that he's gotten so good at gunning the engine and burning rubber, maybe he drives around only late at night when there aren't too many cops out and he can show off to Claudia as much as he likes.

I can't stay in this apartment a minute longer. I peer out the window. The court is dull and darkish, deserted because it's still the lunch hour, and in the distance I can hear a menacing drumroll of thunder. There have been hints of approaching storms many times during this endless hot spell, but they've never come to anything. Might today be the day for the heavens to open? Even the empty benches and the cracked concrete paths around the scraggly garden patches look as though they're panting for rain.

I change my sweat-stained tee-shirt for a fresh one and softly make my way downstairs. I don't know how I'm going to sneak a look at the parking lot. I could see it clearly from Rosalie's apartment. But of course nobody's home and the door's locked, so that's impossible.

The last thing I want to do is run into Alex Kirby. I do want him to know that I'm responsible for what he finds in the front seat of his car. I just don't want him to see me spying on him before he finds it. Yet, how I would love to be able to watch. What's the good of plotting a terrific revenge if you can't see your long-time tormentor being tormented, shuddering and squirming, retching and recoiling in deep horror?

Mrs. Hofmeier's apartment is the first one in Rosalie's row and the closest to ours. Even though it's on the ground floor, she, too, of course has a perfect view of the parking lot from her rear windows. Staying very close to the side of the building, I move slowly, very slowly, along the brick wall toward the back. If only I had eyes that could slide around the corner into the parking lot without the rest of me coming into view.

A flash of lightning stabs the lowering sky and is followed by a deeper roll of thunder. I freeze momentarily against the building wall. The thundery growl dies to a soft rumble. But just as I am about to move again there is a sharp *rat-tat-tat* directly over my head. Instinctively I jump away from the direction of the sound.

When I turn to look up, I see that I've been standing

below a partially opened casement window. It is a window in Mrs. Hofmeier's apartment and Mrs. Hofmeier herself is leaning partway out, her sharp bony finger still on the glass.

My stomach does a flip-flop. The biggest gossip in the court, the leader of all the wagging tongues, has spotted me moving suspiciously beneath her window. What possible reason can I give?

Mrs. Hofmeier is looking directly at me with piercing eyes. Yet she says nothing, only taps again, although less loudly, on the glass. I notice that her majestic head of white hair is disarranged, hanging in wisps around her sagging features. The whites of her eyes are more veined than usual and her color is even pastier and paler than yesterday when I was on my way to meet Duncan. There seems to be a tinge of blueness at her lips.

"Oh yes, Mrs. Hofmeier," I whisper huskily. "Was there something you wanted?"

The bony finger reaches around the glass of the casement and emerges on the outside of the window. It trembles slightly as it slowly turns on itself and curves into a beckoning semicircle. "Come. Come inside," Mrs. Hofmeier says in a choked, gasping voice. "Door's open. C . . . come."

I stand there uncertainly for a moment. Mrs. Hofmeier looks so much like the witch in *Hansel and Gretel* that I feel a little like Gretel being enticed into the gingerbread house. I've never been in Mrs. Hofmeier's apartment before. But something tells me that she is in trouble. Even yesterday she looked peculiar to me as she lay back in her folding chair, still wearing her nightgown and complaining of the lack of air to breathe.

I nod and hurry around to the entrance to the apartment. The sky is getting much darker now and, as I mount the stoop, there's another arrowlike flash of lightning.

Sure enough the door is unlocked. Neighbors have probably been looking in on Mrs. Hofmeier yesterday and today while she's not been feeling well. I pass swiftly through the rooms, heading for the rear bedroom from which Mrs. Hofmeier called to me.

As I enter the room, my first instinct is to look for Mrs. Hofmeier at the window. But she's no longer there. I see that Mrs. Hofmeier's bed is placed directly beneath the window and I realize she must have been kneeling on it as she leaned out, trying to attract the attention of whoever might be passing.

The bed itself is so rumpled that my eye searches it for some moments expecting to see Mrs. Hofmeier's white face and hair against the pillows. The bed, however, is empty. To my horror, Mrs. Hofmeier is lying in a heap on the floor beside it. Her eyes are wide open. She seems to stare, unseeing, at the ceiling. From her lips comes a strange involuntary sound, a mixture of eerie moaning and dry, husky rattling.

"Mrs. Hofmeier!" I scream. "What's wrong?"

The only response I get is an ear-splitting crack of thunder that seems to come from directly overhead. I scream again in pure shock. Mrs. Hofmeier does not stir. Has she fainted or is she dead? I kneel down and grab one of her hands. It's icy and clammy. As I turn it over so I can try to find her pulse, I notice that her fingertips are discolored with the same bluish tinge as her lips. I grope desperately for a flutter of beats in the bulging veins of Mrs. Hofmeier's wrist. My own heart is pounding loudly, but I can't locate her pulse. By now, heavy drops of rain have begun thumping at the windows and a strong wind is hurling itself into the room through the open casement.

I must get help, and quickly. I step over the motionless figure of Mrs. Hofmeier and climb onto her bed. The window that faces on the passageway connecting the court and the parking lot, and through which she called to me, reveals only a slashing rain. I catch a faceful of wetness and close the window rapidly. Again stepping carefully over Mrs. Hofmeier, I dash over to the rear window of the bedroom, the one that looks directly on to the parking lot.

A lone figure is racing toward the parked cars. I yank open the window. "Help!" I yell as loudly as I can. The pelting rain and machine-gunlike thunder claps are stronger than ever. The figure keeps on going. "Help!" I shout again, straining to put the strength of my entire being into my voice. "Please, please. Turn back!"

And even as I'm pleading, "Turn back!" with so much urgency, I know who I'm calling out to. I think I knew it from the beginning. The figure crossing the parking lot, hurrying away from me in the rain and heading toward the cars, is Alex Kirby.

I scream hoarsely one more time and now, at last, he seems to have heard me. He turns and stands very still, gazing in confusion toward the rear window of Mrs. Hofmeier's apartment.

"Here," I shout, waving my arms around like a windmill. "At Mrs. Hofmeier's. Hurry!"

Alex's hair is plastered to his head by the rain. The ends straggling into his eyes are dripping beads of water onto his nose and chin. His drenched shirt is clinging to his skin. He comes in the front door shivering, hunching his shoulders, and rubbing his hands together. His eyes flick across my face in brief, slightly embarrassed recognition.

"What's up?" he asks in an impersonal tone.

"It's Mrs. Hofmeier," I say, hurrying back to where she's lying, as still as when I found her. I kneel down beside her and glance up at Alex. "A heart attack maybe. She just called me in a few minutes ago. I don't know what to do."

Alex sinks to the floor. He reaches for her wrist, he puts his ear to her chest, he checks the whites of her eyes, he parts her lips and peers into her mouth.

"Blue," I say, pointing to her lips. "Her fingers, too. I think I heard somewhere that that's a sign of heart failure."

Alex looks where I've indicated. He brushes back her hair and checks her ear lobes. They, too, look bluish. His movements are surprisingly gentle, swift, and sure.

"Let's get her on the bed," I suggest. Mrs. Hofmeier is so heavy, though, I wonder if we can even manage her between us.

"No!" Alex commands. "Moving her's no good." He points toward the bed. "Get a coupla pillows and some rolled-up sheets to prop up her head. And a blanket to cover her." Alex is already carefully lifting the upper part of Mrs. Hofmeier's body, supporting her back and head against his chest.

I rush around collecting what we need to make Mrs. Hofmeier comfortable on the floor. We straighten out her legs and lift one arm from behind her back where it must have fallen when she collapsed.

Alex rises to his feet. "Watch her," he says. "See she stays propped. Don't let her head fall to one side."

"Where are you going?" I ask in a panicky voice. I'm afraid he'll leave me alone with her and I realize I need him here.

"Find the phone," he mumbles. "None in here. Maybe in the kitchen."

I'm surprised Alex noticed. I haven't even had a chance yet to think where the phone might be. "You're going to call an ambulance, right?"

"Yup," he says. "The volunteer outfit'll get here the fastest. I know some of the fellows. My brother's on the corps. She needs oxygen. Might just make it to the hospital."

A few seconds later Alex is back. He checks Mrs. Hofmeier again with the same quick, expert motions. Then he gets to his feet, folds his arms, and stares down at her.

I'm still on the floor beside Mrs. Hofmeier.

"Will she . . . live?" I ask hesitantly.

He shrugs and makes a face. "Who knows?" he says glumly. "Some do, some don't. Even a doctor couldn't tell you."

"How . . ." I ask, "how come you know all this first-aid stuff, like what signs to look for, what to do? I . . . I just don't."

"Ahh," he says, "it ain't nothing. I hang around the volunteer ambulance guys a lot. It comes . . . natural."

All this time Alex has hardly looked at me. He's kept his eyes fixed on Mrs. Hofmeier. Yet we are having a conversation. And I can tell he's feeling pride in his efficiency and know-how. I've been just about useless in the face of an emergency, and he's had the chance to shine. Everyone likes to shine, at least once in a while. I think of Neil and his part-time lifesaving job at the beach. Probably he doesn't get enough chances to shine. I guess Alex doesn't get nearly as many as he'd like either.

The wail of a siren is heard over the now steady plopping of the rain.

"They're here," Alex announces. He starts for the front door.

I leap up and grab his arm. "Wait," I say. "There's something I need to know. Where were you going when I called you?"

He gives me a surprised look. "Had to get something from the car," he says. A soft smirk spreads across his face. "The water gun. Belongs to Claudia's kid brother. Promised to give it back." He wags his head in an admission of guilt. "Okay, sorry about that. It was just a gag, like all the other stuff. Didn't mean no harm. You shouldn't take everything so personal."

I gaze at him steadily, searching out his eyes. They're gray green, a very odd color against his sallow, tanned skin. "I'm sorry too," I say, thinking of what Alex is going to find in his car when he finally goes to retrieve Claudia's brother's water gun.

I manage to hold his attention a moment longer. I'd like to make a confession. Yet I'm torn. All I can do is gulp hard and repeat, "I'm *really* sorry, Alex." This is the first time I've said his name to his face.

It's clear Alex has no idea what I'm talking about. And I'm becoming more and more overwhelmed with confusion.

"I'm afraid it's too late to do anything about . . . about . . ." I can't bring myself to finish the sentence. I shrug my shoulders in a mixture of hopelessness and hope. "But . . . but maybe," I stammer, "when you've had a chance to think it all over, you'll . . . understand."

Alex gives me a thoroughly baffled look as the ambulance crew bursts in the door.

I turn to glance one last time at poor Mrs. Hofmeier. Will she ever know, I wonder, the part she played in putting an end to my very short career as a horror queen? Even if she recovers—and I truly hope she does—I don't suppose I'll ever tell her.

17

Changes

IT'S A CLEAR, sparkling afternoon. Playful waves are splashing at the shore, tossing up joyous sprays of foam. The air is laced with cool, salty breezes. Rosalie and I are sitting side by side on the beach, *our* beach back home.

"And you never told me," Rosalie singsongs in a teasing voice.

"Never told you what?" I demand almost indignantly. It seems to me I've told Rosalie everything. I've told her about the revenge I planted in Alex Kirby's car, about the afternoon at Mrs. Hofmeier's with Alex, about how I felt my act of horror had backfired after a new and surprisingly different side of Alex Kirby was revealed to me. And, yes, I've even told her all about Duncan and me.

Rosalie gazes off into the distance. It's been over a week now since the day of Mrs. Hofmeier's heart attack, and this weekend Mom has driven Rosalie and me down to the shore for a couple of days. Mom, too, now knows everything that's happened and she's reacted with shock, relief, understanding, and humor—in that order. "A problem-solver to make your old mother proud." That was what Mom called me.

"You never told me about your adorable *brother*," Rosalie retorts now. "He's quite a hunk. How could you have kept him under wraps all through our friendship, Marleen?"

I shrug. I guess maybe I haven't told Rosalie everything after all. I haven't told her about how angry I was with Neil and his girlfriend, Yolanda, after my last visit home. I haven't told her how at times Neil and Alex seemed so much alike to me that they fused in my mind, and I built up even more anger toward each of them.

Now on this magical weekend toward the end of summer, when the atmosphere seems full of both relief and promise, things appear to have changed a lot. For one thing, Yolanda is gone. When I sourly asked Neil about her shortly after we arrived, he shook his mop of blond, sun-streaked hair and told me she was a "twit" and they had called it quits weeks ago.

Even better than that, Neil had seemed as glad to see me as Pop had. He'd slung a loving brotherly arm around my shoulder, squeezed me tightly, and called me "stranger." I was astonished and, of course, immediately felt guilty. The whole world was turning upside down for me. But in a nice way.

Which Neil had been the real Neil, which the real Alex? How hard it is to ever really get a permanent fix on anything or anyone in this life.

"Anyhow," Rosalie goes on, "I really like your whole family. Your mom, your pop." She turns her head and gazes up the beach to where my parents are sitting together on an umbrella-shaded blanket, their heads bent over some papers they're studying and on which Pop makes notations from time to time.

"You should be proud of them." Is Rosalie scolding me just a little? "Your mom is a really talented person and gutsy, too. She's taken her life in hand. And your pop is big enough not to feel outdone. He's proud of how well her sweatwear business is going. Even if it means having a different life-style for a while, he's being supportive. He's backing her all the way."

I guess Rosalie *is* giving me a lecture. She's trying to tell me she admires my family not only because it's "different," but because it's truly special in a good way. So, there too, I guess I was seeing only the darker side of things when I bitterly accused Bobbie of splitting up the family.

Rosalie leans forward and grabs her bare ankles. She's wearing a bright red jersey tank suit that shows up the creamy whiteness of her skin. An enormously wide-brimmed straw hat protects her from the sun and makes her look, when she's standing, a little like a two-legged mushroom.

"Know what I'm going to do this afternoon?" she queries me with a wicked leer. "I'm going to get your handsome Greek god of a brother to take me out in the catamaran. Wanna bet?"

"Rosalie," I reply, "I'm sure you can accomplish anything you set your heart on doing. I'm not betting." Already I can see Rosalie and Neil bouncing over the waves in the lightweight double-hulled boat the lifeguards use to investigate any trouble they might spot out past the breakers.

I never before put Rosalie and Neil together in my mind. But, come to think of it, she might be just the

142

right challenge for him. Short and pudgy though she is, especially under her huge floppy hat, she's actually no mushroom. Her figure is curvy and intriguing in its skintight red suit. To Neil, after a whole string of Yolandas, most of them "twits," Rosalie may well prove to be an exotic plant.

"Oh, you sly fox," Rosalie exclaims, getting to her feet and brushing sand from her thighs. "You haven't done so badly yourself. All those sneaky get-togethers with Duncan." She wiggles a shoulder at me. "I'm really *awfully* sorry I was cramping your style."

I squint up at Rosalie, shielding my face against the sun with my hand.

"Please," I remind her. "Only one sneaky get-together. You know about all the others."

It's true that I've seen Duncan just about every day since that first morning over at the Weller place. I've never told him, though, about the two plastic bags I dragged away next morning and emptied into Alex Kirby's car in my attempt to get even with him. And I've pledged Rosalie to secrecy.

I can't imagine what Duncan would think if he knew. I'm so overcome by how intelligent and caring and sensitive he is. I never dreamed any boy could be like that. I don't want to risk spoiling anything while we're still so new to each other. Maybe later. I don't know.

I'm full of mixed feelings even now whenever I think about what I did. Was it really so wrong to have nourished my revenge fantasy to the point of fulfilling it? How could anyone else know how I felt, being humiliated over and over again by Alex, and by Alex and Claudia? True, it had all started out with Alex making fun of my mother. But that was something Mom didn't even pay any attention to. So *I* soon became the victim, the target, "it."

I couldn't go on taking that from Alex. I just couldn't.

Rosalie's all finished brushing the sand from her legs. She takes off her hat—it comes from THE GENTLE PAUSE, which is certainly no surprise—and places it on the beach towel beside me.

"Well," she says boldly, "I'm off to tangle with your gorgeous brother over at the lifeguard station. Wish me luck."

I wave her off indifferently. She'll do fine. I know it.

The truly amazing thing was the way Alex reacted to the sickening sight and awful stench in his car. Maybe it was my cryptic warning just before they took Mrs. Hofmeier away that helped prepare him to a degree. Maybe he actually saw my point a little and respected me for hitting back at last. Maybe he even thought he deserved what he got.

Anyhow, I saw him crossing the court two days later. Mom had returned from her solitary trip to the shore the night before and I was getting ready to load the car for the sweatwear party that she and I had scheduled for Friday evening. I had just gotten the latest hospital report on Mrs. Hofmeier from our downstairs neighbor and I thought I ought to tell Alex.

I walked right up to him, although not without butterflies in my stomach and a mouth as dry as the Sahara. He halted when he saw me approaching and all he said was, "Hi."

"I . . . I don't know if you heard," I mumbled, "but I thought you'd like to know. Mrs. Hofmeier's doing much better today. They think she's going to pull through. You . . . probably saved her life.''

Alex just stared at me for a few seconds. "Yeah," he said. "That's good. Hope she makes it."

I half turned to go. I could see that talking to Alex was never going to be easy. But at the last minute I swung back. I just had to know. "How . . . how's your car?"

To my surprise, he grinned. Then he just stood there shaking his head at me in an up-and-down motion. "Some mess," he said, with almost no expression at all in his voice. But he kept on nodding. I had the oddest feeling that he was thinking to himself that what I had done to him was kind of neat, something that he wouldn't have minded doing to somebody himself.

Rosalie has reached the lifeguard station by now and I scramble to my feet to get a better view. She's looking up at Neil in his tall seat. I can see her head bobbing as she delivers her taunting yet commanding request. Neil will fall under her spell, I know, just as I have. He'll do exactly as she wishes.

I'm glad I met Rosalie. It's interesting that it was Mrs. Hofmeier who brought us together. What was it Rosalie had said to me when I told her that because of what happened with Alex at Mrs. Hofmeier's I was definitely ending my career as a horror queen?

She had said, "I'm glad." And then she had delivered one of her mysterious pronouncements. As with all the others, I didn't know if it was a famous quotation or if she had made it up herself on the spur of the moment. So I asked her.

"This one," she said, "is practically a quote. But I fixed it up a little to suit your particular case, Marleen." And then, so it would really sink in I guess, she closed her eyes and very slowly and solemnly repeated it.

"She who studieth revenge," Rosalie intoned, "keeps her own wounds green."

And I think she was right.

About the Author

LILA PERL has written more than thirty books, both fiction and nonfiction, most of them for young adults. She was awarded a B.A. degree from Brooklyn College and has taken graduate courses at Teachers College, Columbia University and the School of Education at New York University. Also available as Archway paperbacks are her popular titles: *Annabelle Starr, E.S.P.; Hey, Remember Fat Glenda?; Me and Fat Glenda;* and *Pieface and Daphne.*

Inspired through the years by her two children, now grown, Ms. Perl currently lives with her husband in Beechhurst, New York. She says of her motivation in creating *Marleen, the Horror Queen* that she loved the challenge of writing a "realistic horror story" and explains that "Many of us have felt, at times, like the helpless victim of a mean, taunting enemy. We've ached to get even in some wild, dramatic and thoroughly delicious way. It was fun translating Marleen's thoughts of revenge into action."